I0522408

THE BOXCAR BOP

T.C. PESCATORE

ISBN: 978-1-64255-916-3
Run Amok Books, 2018
First Edition

Printed in the U.S.A.

for Joe, Milo & Otis

to all bums lost in time
& left out of focus

Music,

Maestro,

Please.

An Enchanted Opening and Closing ceremony

On an oft quoted day in American world history when that famous fissure in reality stabilized there were two figures left over jumped the cliff was the term on the other side that was gone now so the term making no sense was retired on this side tho no one had ever uttered it so in most every and any way it was an empty gesture and these two figures always moving in bright multicolored that is patch brown dusty multicolored plaid shadows set out to better the world they'd found themselves in.

There was a bullhorn stenogra-narrator somewhere wrote this one this origin story down really loud with that feedback scratch loop just so that when you thought you were listening right you hadn't caught the gist at all and rolling back off the tip of your ear it sounded off into the blue spackled night like this one you're watching now from your beds children

Test—ah—ha—right—Testing
out in Oklahoma okie blue plains of American
grassland fatland cows mooing to the milky
setting sun of midwest time—
a test and the paper moves
gurgles—marches into the marching distance
toward thirsting
MISSILES or APOCalypseS of
hourly doom coming each hour
counting each hour on
branches missing arms as no branches
would venture————————
————————galloping from the distance to
the foreground an underground—
a narration—

"We're about to venture a journey," Kenneth the taller of the two slouch shouldered heroes moaned, "A journey—to see what all this here robin's egg world's got to shit and trot my man, got to off-off-offer! a-a-a pardon me-what'd'ya call it? A~~~~it's a type ah ah ah ahah!? A genre bend ah-ah come on you know a great Ody-odd-uh, let's see, a ja-ja-ja-J—"

But as an act a sheer twist of fate Braun the shorter of the two slouch shouldered heroes happened to go deaf for that split second at the pop of the fracture's last gasps and final closure and missed Ken's obvious point and he leapt into the air with some jagged rhyming vestigial idea, he heard jazz in his ears buzzing like the ear phone hydrogen release aftermath on your iphone under your pillow tucked safely away and he stuck he struck one great grand idea finger into the air going, "Ken! Indeed...a gurney is what we need!"

"A gurney." "No"

"no?" "Agh."

"Yes" "No?"

"yes" "ah"

"YES" "yes."

"no!" "A stretcher!" This is how it became all confused. A stretcher was not a gurney, not a journey not a—you see where this is going where there was no time to argue before—

"Stretcher," Ken finally agreed, albeit hesitantly. And grabbing both ends himself Braun vibrating at multplicit frequencies ran in circles upon circles not very fast and Ken jazzed 8-heads high above the crowd yet to arrive—the rabble just beyond the cover of hill yonder and the field yonder and the corn of Nebraska high Iowa hell hidden now beyond the pale blue smoldering fog of the smiling Adirondacks—there wasn't a ticket left or to be sold to this intergalactic inter-dimensional dance, this cosmically awake event, this meteorically seismic wake. All over the world news of the fissure had spread through 24 hour news broadcasting world cable websites on tv screen touch remote heaven where the eyes of all the brain mashed public looked on agape, the many faced journalist and tele-journalists and inter-blog-journalists were setting course, they were barreling down *en masse en massacre en route* to Pulitzer-pantomime-Parrott gun prizes winning glory hoary whorey futures, they were gonna flesh out the story stretch out the story until it was rolled out red and deflated homogenized and packaged to the nearest decimal point for ratings 7 billion strong.

"You are not al*ooooo*ne," Ken prepared his speech while looking down at Braun who like the sprig of wheat hanging from his mouth was lounging on the grassy ground unconcerned hands behind head elbows going against the vanishing line.

That's when the idea hit him again. It was an again idea that had left and come back around to become a brand fucking new idea that hadn't ever even dared to have made the rounds the first time. That original grand idea, that first scratch of an idea, that fire wielding, paint brush brandishing thought, the idea that could give birth to human, the frontier, the beyond.

(Braun)(Ken not saying this just nodding in general direction of the rotting fossilized gurney and his friend looking up into oh so painted blue sky and heavy thick clouds whistling some lost tune of forgetfulness and regret) "A journey, I mean to embark on a journey, of course, to find what's left out there to find, to see all this land has to offer us!" Braun, torn from his silent daydream, by the words from the mouth he himself had spoken, landed on his feet where he'd been standing the whole time. TWO fingers into the air this time.

"Alright, but holy *holy* moley hel if that wasn't what I said to you exactly when we got exactly here in this low down milky farawayspace not two or 20 or 60 minutes earth time ago, you gotta pay more attention when I'm beating you to the punch," Kenneth bemoaned, bobbed, bobbing his head to the string vibrations and the percussion swells of the invisible sounds and smells of the lower dimensional burst, "and now, now my boy, the most essential task! We gotta find a ride that'll suit our merry band before those flags go up and the spectators abound."

So they made ready to push through the crowds they knew would be forming—

see: this 4D author's space omnipotent view not only were the news vans bearing down but spilling from the houses alight now in the town, many tiny feet pounding, many wheels of the countryside wheeling, thinking another UFO cah-rash, another blue rose, the caravans of the east and west reeling, there wasn't going to be a hotel left standing when this universe-con began or ended, no food nor lodging to be found stadiums turned right over and sports teams left sprawled out number by number over the fertile athletic grounds—they would be like translating tornado expressions underwater and gone nobody sure if they'd seen or left or been there the whole time or hadn't arrived, just sequential images on the brain caught between filth which is the sensation one gets when time sinks into itself and slows down, it's like an Olympic swimmer dunked into a river of pure Canadian maple syrup, existence grinding to a halt—here a compilation of what the merged masses would have thought they'd seen, and what you perhaps doubtlessly originally saw on the screen

"tweed jacket, fedora cap

no no

get it, he did and he did

they did—

they them they both did—

it's two things
honest to goodness
two bodies
standing single file
astride death's horse
no death *it-self*
no
Side-
by-
Side
What you'd consider men
In this way of seeing
But was much more
Random phased
down
2twotootwo2
upon death's ugly cattle's head

the little boys that love them
throw persimmon colored flowers at their feet—

the little girls that love them
write little love poems that, little, begin—

a piano on gory blue shores
where no river goes and
black hats
of
an age—
any age—
nobody knows

already they're here in the image of a child mind—"

"We are the old things that must die and go away to be reborn."

Imagine that on the evening news heard everywhere at once (pome) 'cause it was accompanied by a blank screen and monotone voice the same voice same AP newscaster reporter's voice spilling the juice for each company owned by the same somebody and nobody outside of the top got it and good grand gelato what else was there to new do but give in to the belief that there hadn't been first contact at all with men from another dimensional music space, it was too easy to sleep and remember the only remnant, the only physical evidence found:

There was this little boygirl girlboy who followed their footprints in the fields who patted and petted the heads of hungry sparrows and groaned of pharmacologically implanted pains he was a boy she was a girl without father or mother or sister or brother an orphan child who'd seen all the mess on TV and planned to see for himherself if inter-dimensional wayfaring writers could truly, in this gritty realm of realism and washed out colors, exist. S/He turned off CNNFOXLite in the fields and the prairie dogs woke up after 300 years, jumped and followed behind, and the vultures swooped happily full and content in the charming brain waves of hisher sighs. Bringing peace with her, he wandered into town a lost little one a lost ideal a lost populace running round unseeing what s/he saw—these two classical clowns.

An entire life—three entire lives in actuality—leading up to this unappreciated, underappreciated 3-in-hole-in-1 meeting in the godhead of space. Ken recognized the kid; Braun doffed his cap in respect. The child unaware that the future had cut into the past simply raised THREE fingers and then let them pass, choking out no words not a single useless word beyond the mutter of the a vulture on her shoulder (who always muttered pitilessly) and the prairie dog he'd named mouse sleeping z-z-zing tucked in his hobo sock.

When the world sped back up to catch itself in time in the place of the rift and the stretcher and the threadbare men there was left instead the little girl with no name and no parents and no home, just his animal spirits the clothes she'd stolen to keep himself warm against the mist and spray of Atlantic crashing waves.

The paparazzi fell upon this confused scene and in one hideous hilarious swoop of scoop and cameras flashing, and feathers and fur and cries, they devoured him whole (in made for teevee movie time, in news flash time, in trending topics time) spitting out in chunks of hours of headline clickbait schemes, her guiltless childhood ivory bones—dream a dream ah dream a doh a dream oh dear ah dream.

—and it was this sacrificial action, this Christ-on-the-cross-like-joan-on-the-pyre-like-intervention, this Manichaean-light-like-martyrdom, which gave them the time (Kenneth and Braun) to search the country side for their desired ride—

See
they *had* to go
but
no *way* of going
no 54' Cadillac sunning in the breeze
not even a tandem peddle bike which up
until now had been the vehicle of choice on
their world between the stars = they had no way to go,
no way to when no way to be = they were stuck = an end
with no means

"SO what you're saying if I can get at this straight…is the first part of this journey…" Braun continued from a thought that had been banging around in his head independently, "You're saying here now that now here we…"

"Yes the very first and least thing you want to say, that most important part…" Ken supported noddingly rockingly.

"Is to find us a …"

"*Aye...*"

"A ride..."

"Aha! And not just any damn ride mind you…"

"it's gotta have Style."

"grace."

"iNcoherence."

"*l'amour.*"

"Beauty *ugliness* flavor"

"plastics metals rubbers leathers"

"wings jet engines railings jokes"

"food blankets clothing dryer bells"

"wheels wells gas tanks beads"

"Now you're getting it," Ken tapped Braun on the chin and looked longingly into the dead windows of the dead town they faced, "We're on the outskirts now but about to dive into this shit. It's time to build and break and rend, time to get this baby of a show on the continental ticking road."

"That little chil' won't hold off the crowds for long—" Braun sniggered feigningly unconcerned looking into the same dead windows of that same dead town only differently because he was a different man. Thing that're different is new draw ire bile sinew and regret.

"Yeah, I can see what you mean," Ken snapped his fingers to emphasize his pondering mind, "We'll have to play this game fast, androgyny is a bitch to these neutral dicks."

"The fastest. *Najbrzi.*"

"What's the fastest game we've ever played?" He asked knowingly.

"That time out on old highway B-67 stringer by dusty shelves and bat-wing doors if I'm not mistaken it was in universe 7mnT," Braun drew into the sand of the mud of the dirt on the dirt road shoulder with a stick he'd picked up not too far back near the last evergrowth tree in the known universe, "And I never am."

And Ken rolling his eyes, flipped his dangling platinum coin, the one with a striking resemblance to a pocket watch crushed by the rolling tonnage of a locomotive train and let it fall into the collar of his open coat, saying, "Ah, m'boy, I'd say this is going to have to be a fucking hell of a lot faster than that if we ever wanna get this show on the dang road."

All this was done under the hot eyes of god's Midwestern sun.

How they got the car and other things you need to know; including but not limited to an old song ain't heard no more

'Of all the gol' dang universes in all the tripping falling hypertime realities of this spinning bluey-green sphere, he *had* to collapse into this one,' Braun thought out loud as he wrote it down to be read by eyes and minds outside his conceptually abstracted view and according to the walking shaking typewritten pages in your hands. He'd just stepped into his third floor office, (Braun Rodman PIE, Private Investigator *Extraordinaire* that is, Private Panoptical EYE licensed by the state of new york in that great tired city of new york [sic] the big apple never sleeps—no fooling) when he felt that presence beyond the door. Waiting. So he huffed, yeah, and he thought, oh the hell with it I never bothered to hire an administrative assistant (secretary is archaic term) and nicking the door softly with his foot, took a step in, the mosaic window cut out the door frame with Arial gold letters (he was feeling sans serif that day when he ordered the damn nameplates) offering our *homme fatale* seated inside anonymity until that final second when all was laid bare and two figures on the shot put earth hurled by some unknown force stood revealed. Smoking and musing to himself, he turned musingly slowly in the direction of the grizzled tweed wearing detective behind him (now you see we've altered perspective in this grand game)

Kenneth, cigarette dangling limply from his mouth, thin trail of smoke curling round his dark curls curling to the ceiling to disperse about craggy white ceiling of the cold water flat retrofitted into space-age noir-age office space, nodded serenely, carelessly at the figure standing before him batting barely there eyelashes over and over heavy lusty eyes.

"Mr. Rodman," spoken coldly through the hot smoke of the ash flashed on his right hand.

"Why hello there...eh heheheh, Mr. *Rodman*, I presume? We talked earlier on the phone, yes? Now, what can I do for you?" Braun responded, moving around to situate himself behind his desk—in front of his chair—on which he thought about sitting, hesitated, then decided it was probably right to sit as his guest was sitting and from a quick lazy limp handed perusal of the *Revelations of Dr. Modesto* now stuck in the far pocket of his desk that's appropriately apparently what you were supposed to do as a right sycophant in an effort to make a meaningful connect—in this formalized formulaic hardboiled business setting—he exhaled sat leaning back breathing blinking taking out from the desk his own silver pressed case of hand rolleds popping it open reaching in for a sprig placing the twisted tobacco colored stem in his mouth lighting puffing lighting puffing. Now wait for it https://www.KennethRodmansDimeStoreDetectiveNovelPlot Pitch.com—

"I got a look see, I got someone following me, some spectre in the violet night, some phantom unseen. They jacked my car, sure as I'm hell-bent on sitting here, roughed me up, trashed my pad too, know where I live," all this in cool, monotone, something fishy Braun thought, something ain't right about this, but he rested quietly waiting, still, smoke burnt off the end of sweet north caroline smells, "This is how I see it, Rodman to Rodman, maybe a relation sir, I don't know (nobody calls me sir ya cur but go on) there's someone in this reality out to get me see I'm shifting through dimensional space on my way to the coast and now I'm stuck here on the right side when I need to be somewhere else, see on the left, I'm here like I say and you see, on the right, that's not right. I only got two weeks a' travel this fine foreign land scratchin' my head, see, I gotta move or I'll be dying stuck here in your two ten cent type layout all letters times new roman words feeding on the eyes of *whatever* voyeurs come upon this space. Dammit, you gotta see I don't have time! Of course you came highly recommended..." (I don't take compliments well, well, I am all compliments on my yelp page of infinite stars, no case I haven't solved no perp I haven't nailed scribble-scratched Braun to himself on the notepad's lined face, that's a shit line but it'll make it into the memoir for sure, hah! Kenneth still talking I missed a whole fucking twenty minutes of this sobbing soaked wet tale that I ain't buying for a second some odd thing being off about the whole blasted set up nod yeah professional just like that).

You're able to picture this all in black and white seas of gray, awash on the colorless shore, your car drives up parks in front of the screen here's what it looks like:

Behind the classic 1920s Casablanca(o) desk, tweed jacket [important first look at our proud heroes so pay close attention] modern fit cut in at the ribs underarm colored like that old couch in your aunt's house cross-hatched with plaid patterns bright orange and black snuck in some green, gloves cut off at the fingers, black fedora sitting about long auburn hair, full beard, large hazel eyes, olive corduroy pants (this is suddenly familiar) beat up sambas seems outta place touch hem helm with style but what the bloody hell it's 1969 somewhen somewhile.

Kenneth across, bescarfed in silk, bearded, ponytailed deep wine dark black hair like greek oceans long ago, tweed jacket too, matching but umber brown, burnt umber, no gloves, callused hands for guitar strings, beat up jeans, full black converse shoes. Office is perfect square, no pictures on walls, minimal, hardwood floors desk empty but for pen/notepad/sickly looking lamp emitting cagey tired yellow light/typewriter rundown old remington been lugged chugged snapped pounded full since birth ribbon almost bled out. Everything else you got your own imagination, just think what gene autry would say to humphrey bogart, this here red dress, joan crawford—now to continue. Kenneth sneaks a look at Braun's moving pen, *hrmmms,* goes on:

"Well I want you to tail these brutes. I knows where they live [sliding a walmart stock photo across the desk] and I ain't too shy to show ya, but they're bad like wild west story bad in fact conjured from old pulp tales of the west in movies that ran all night with hobos sleeping in hovels in the movie theatres of the soul, dig? This ain't no cake'a'walk by any means. There's danger in every corner of this here literary genre, ya?"

Now he's speaking the man's language regardless of the truth in it, "ya peaked my interest n' curiosity both," Braun coughed out smoke gutted lungs, "I'll tell ya what kid, I'm going to take this case, by the hour, free of charge til' I nail the suckers did this, find your shiny ol' ow-toe-moe-beal then it's going to be up to you to answer for the unasked questions I'm yet to be askin'."

"Right, when you get this here thing's a'going pops, I'll be ready to do whatever's asked," Kenneth speaking hip outta turn with the reader pop outta the story this is for a breath to catch to refresh and pause for this italicized intermission for we dive back in and skip on get on to that action chase scene stakeout lamb. wink wink.

Scene shift 24 hours later after various reconnaissance missions too boring too lengthy to leave here but imagine there were chapters and chapters of fist to jaw interrogation and our investigators escaping bloody though with their lives—climbing out windows, dropping teeth, wiping sweat/tears/intrigue what have you from their square iron souls—intact and isn't this just the longest scene shift you ever read but it had to be with all the various lives lived and resurrected and reincarnated gha gha gah now explode to the finale the miserable confrontation the action packed conclusion, here go-oh-oes

Three toughs on corner 1930s corner of the cracked pavement cold water flat tenement housing rise toward sky but still bent and sulking image now shifting under gentrifier's wet-dream outcomes cum-dom kingdoms. These three shadows are not even worth describing think of classic lackey mentality laughing like leather jacketed poorboy cap wearing children of the former decades image distilled in faded photographs of the grand rodeo of how could this be real only so many years ago, photos in the attic silly—it only takes one hundred years to be completely forgotten. Braun and Kenneth in the cafeteria across the street once again sipping stale coffee, once again because they had sipped stale coffee before although you might not have read it previously, watching out glimmer of conversational eye/the score my fine and dandy reader my Dashell Hammet motherfuckers, my writer's soul slavers and it's time to rope us all into this big stakeout fuck noir of a story and find out this mystery 1 2 3 roll camera roll fingers typing, shit—

Braun strolls up to the three leaning on the car like ole time characters, they uneasy, watch as mystery man approaches but retain their cool, just catch him as he pulls up leans on trunk, they're all up by the hood.

"What's the deal, fella," No. 1 goes, trying to sound hard, "You got a problem?"

"Hey, yeah, you got a problem buddy, you're gonna scuff my boy's car, huh uh? That ain't gonna be good for your um pretty face," No. 2 in turn. No. 3 looks on he doesn't look to be in a speaking mode, just slip tightens hold on his brass knuckles, hands in pockets but you can sense the metal on skin unnatural scratch.

"Ya know what," Braun says, "I does," Braun says, with rhythm they ain't used to in this time zone, like Charlie Parker blowing on some kinda sax from the 35th century, it's all cut up and blaring. Scrapping the dirt from his index finger's nail with his teeth, he gets on over the rush of the street adjacent, the rest of the celestial scene, "Yeah, yeah, I got a problem."

Kenneth now saddling up next to him, still coffee cup in hand (must'a stole it from that cafeteria must'a straight walked out with his refill still steaming a'cause it was steaming now in his hand makin' an even bigger affront to the three men on the other side, other end of the old 72 buick (forgot to mention the car I guess, it's black, rusted out, breaks cut, solid angles, old beast of the american road, built for two things chewing up miles and chewing up gas. A real american road devil). Both Rodman smile. The three men smile too, hands in their pockets ready for a go. All is right with the tense about to break world.

There's violence so often in the sad mono-colored iris of man.

Post-It note left on Braun's desk: *This is where you gotta unnerstan' this ain't no genre flick this is being able to cross through narrative time. This is this is this is the original tale you hung on to. This is what was meant from the beginning. You're the mark.*

You're the mark, see? You've been fooled into security of the false sense kind, a play on narrative perception—You've been conned as much as the next man as like the casino fool playing his last hand—this is just a temporary fix, the mini boss fight, the third act of the Hollywoodland play—it stinks like con men smooth talking sway—

Here's the honest truth of the matter spilt out spelled out clad out—

Ragged sounds and music wailing to that crescendo climax finish that Sisyphus summits edge tumbling to the opposite shores of Montezuma, now it's time for the tension wail, the battle cry. Music untold sounds off into the resplendent night.

But that's not how it has to be. 'Course these Rodman boys steal the show steal the car too just move sidewise through space-time take the two front seats, our men pounding the windows won't break, black to red wires hotwires hotwired peddle down to floor engine roar and the cars off headed west on out that city never sleeps ignoring street signs city lines, *that's a stolen car,* Kenneth laughs, *you believe that set up, you believe those suckers thinkin' we was gonna fight?* Braun with the loud heavy guffaw, *pshaw now mister Rodman why would they ever believe something as fool crazy as that? Ha-ha! Didn't you say this was your cahr?* they both going, howling as Manhattan fades as the boroughs become a no-thing in their stead. These lips and dips into the bleed into the story sphere, a singular voice you might hear on empty empire state roads from jersey to here, *never owned one, sir, you really got me going, now, I gotta see what this here Buick can really do! Floor it!*

Kenneth, in the driver's seat (see his hand shake that throttle, drive that sumovabitch low break that bucking bronc's back bend it to the will of the task Lorena ask where this lil' chil' has been) "Braun m'boy it's at times like this streaking out the cityscape I think o' my lost love and hear those angel voices blow for the ocean we're leaving to that ocean we seek to find, that tear between worlds that'll get us home…I ever tol' you about…?"

"Oh no…mot…No…"

Oh my my my my my why why why wait oh
why here it is why oh my oh my why repent repent repent!
Oh ancient days ancient days this song sing song
Is why why ah ah aha hah ahaha ha

And Ken, he goes on to sing, the radio picking up the tune, dials its own response, catching up singing along into the sparkled sour past sad voices stories all wrapped up in bows, Kenneth and the radio arm in arm figuratively metaphorically methodologically ring methodically sing sing sing:

The years creep slowly by, Lorena,
Snow is on the grass again;

Here this automatic shift, spin the next lane and blow—

The sun's low down the sky, Lorena,
The frost gleams where the flowers have been;
But the heart throbs on as warmly now,
As when the summer days were nigh;
Oh! the sun can never dip so low,
A down affection's cloudless sky.

Braun, face screwed up in its brawniest, just goes on through the car window watching side views of rectangular gold fields split by green tracks of unwashed unblemished land, nips at the baleful flask he's pulled from the glove compartment, scratch of strong hard amber liquid oh down the hatch darling down down ow ow now down tha hatch please

A hundred months have passed, Lorena,
Since last I held thy hand in mine;

And felt the pulse beat fast, Lorena,
Though mine beat faster far than thine;
A hundred months, 'twas flowery May,
When up the hilly slope we climbed,
To watch the dying of the day,
And hear the distant church bells chime.

Ah jagged italicized lines and Ken got his own shit blowing Braun gonna let him cry gonna watch as Ohio flashes by in the neck of a flask in the fairy addled mind the green-scape landscape go, voices burn that pit of belly, voices voices—

We loved each other then, Lorena.
More than we ever dared to tell;
And what we might have been, Lorena,
Had but our lovings prospered well.
But then ,'tis past, the years are gone,
I'll not call up their shadowy forms;
I'll say to them, "lost years, sleep on!
Sleep on! Nor heed life's pelting storms."

I'm gonna go stanza by stanza god bliss blush the anchin' lan' Ken is gone now in reverie gotta let this sick stomach chart its course—there's some [sic] but that'd be copyright infringement to alter it—if'n you haven't figured it out yet, Braun scratching down on that dusty moleskin line lined, we set you all up and stole this honest car and now gonna plow wow ow ow ow oh how this lan lan lan land you traverse we just needed the wheels to cast the sigil spell the chaotic whistle well, you get the gist he's writing to himself to readers reading well you see it was some kinda confession E-laborate scheme to pull this reader's mind along to jostle that last shred of trust free from the blood, those kids as type, as letters stretched together to formulate words on, now in confused huddle, wondering what to do as we swing the last corner into the void, a missing car grand theft auto report, their only hope and the admittance that the car was long past inspection dates a tale for the tail end of the purply pasts of horizons rising milky way sprays a

> *story of that past, Lorena,*
> *Alas! I care not to repeat;*
> *They touched some tender chords, Lorena,*

Ack akc akc akc akhs alak hak hak hack

> *They lived, but only lived to cheat.*
> *I would not cause even one regret,*
> *To rankle in your bosom now;*
> *"For if we try we may forget,"*
> *Were words of thine long years ago.*

These lines just ain't for show they got Ken scrapping hard on the wheel leaving finger marks of eternity's wisp on leather heating up showing up showing off bout to traipse the soil of missing Gaul that Ohio dayton land you kin lose your hat in if'n you aren't careful snapping back fotos of signs declared Needmore road, see the resemblance see the ironie irony we ee ee need more road need more highway more gas man flash pan man out Ohioan i-wan indiana illinois man missouri mississippi roar down belly of beastly earth c'mon finish up this sad sweet song so's we can get to the next shift next void sucking black hole oblivion we got hours miles stories space time travel hell to get through Braun can't voice the concern o'er sweet lost lyrics he jus' joins in bellowing

> *Yes, those were words of thine, Lorena,*
> *They are within my memory yet;*
> *They touched some tender chords, Lorena,*
> *Which thrill and tremble with regret.*

'Twas not the woman's heart which spoke,
Thy heart was always true to me;
A duty stern and piercing broke,
The tie that linked my soul with thee.

ee eee nothin' more to say just stanza lines linger one more

sad tearful gasp and we on on on off ov off off here wo we go

both Rodman voices in harmony radio silent invisible the song

blaring on invisible radio wave microwave frequency is only

to cover their tracks but

It matters little now, Lorena,
The past is in the eternal past;
Our hearts will soon lie low, Lorena,
Life's tide is ebbing out so fast.
There is a future, oh, thank God!
Of life this is so small a part,
'Tis dust to dust beneath the sod,
But there, up there, 'tis heart to heart.

curtains ruby red pulled back curtains so we are naked
visible
Inter-dimensional this car car is not a car it's a it's uh it is
this iss iz shifting through unknown
Invisible meta-fictional layers of scrape-scape spilling space
and stomachaches

"Git it outtar space," Kenneth rockets
on to the deck of the ship shit see it's a spaceship
reality no longer rusted rig of
jalopy four wheel kicks,
and Braun's jackhammering while sipping
coffee from dispenser built into the deck,
"Git it outta spacer
and let me flip the
switch that *goes*—," Kenneth goes
until the boats off gray and rocking
in the shredded green
of the heartland we've well forgotten's there,

"We lost--oh but we're lost, *O Lost!*
how can it be, I put the cabin
together barehanded, just like
your directions say—" Braun
barehandedly laments (sarcastically?)

—"but it's finished!" they finish
together, taking turns as captain, second mate, steward,
cook, gunner, oar-er, smasher,
basher, dancer, crasher, musician, sleeper, muse, drunk,
writer, captain, general, admiral, second hand, rower, rover,
captain, captain, captain,
skier

there's a million hands shaking in front of them
a million bombs blasting below them a million thoughts
thinking before them, thinking it's thinking keeps them
afloat
but it ain't see, it's floating keeps them thinking they're afloat
or
the sound of a million hands basket weaving,

"Higher now or we'll hit the clouds...!" either of them say--
one's got
finger-less gloves, the other wine, the other wine and the
other
shoes shined--O shined with finger-less gloves under the
twisting
acorn hobo trees canary blossoms cherry bark fissure, "Keep
it on the sun,"
Braun, now captain, deadpans, "turn out for dinner you
swine!" Kenneth roars
like the cooks of all old ghost ships roar "and if anything at
all makes sense
you'll all go blind blind blind blind har har har—" and he
slops the slop with the joy of a slop chef on all the clean
white plates,

"don't forget the key limes in a chant on the ocean-less
oceans of chime"--and the musicians kick in with
the lead on the first line and the sun was pink raspberries
over the under clouds

as they say, and the sailing behemoth cut through, and the
boys ate a hearty meal
from the cook about to be first mate and the captain about
cleaning the latrine—
the merry-go-gg-go-go-round boat of the same name,

"Set'ahr a'course!" neither yelled, "for starry shores
and apple trees! O' set a course for snow and berries and
cosmic bees!" cleaning
captaining scrubbing ordering, killing, writing, talking
singing whistling being, finishing,

"For
WORLDS AND
IMAGES and skies
sorely known!

This ain't jazz, this is life on the miss-uh-ssippi.

All aboard--the steamer RODMAN U.S.S

making all LO-CAL StopS."

and the quaking eternal and expanding universe shook to its
oldest black hole super nova bones—

The big Prairie sky and return of the child nipping at the heels of the world-sphere going going going

"Step right up step right up gather 'round gather round ladies gentle-ladies men gentlemen boys girls children grandchildren gather your mammas papas mom-moms pop-pops grab'em all and gather round take a seat in the circle 'round the wagon wheel lissen here listen hear! Your eyes will pop your ears will sing your nose well, your nose I swear will swell will swill to this sweet smell this scintillating sensational superficial supra-fictional spectacular!

"Lean back relax knell peel heal reel let Ole shyster Kenneth take you on an adventure a word journey a trek to the very gates of ecstasy heaven, let this trick be the sound be the soothing spiel of your impoverished famished, hungry as you please, soul!

"Round up round'em up here we here we go quiet now quiet your attention here on these eyes bubbling over the brim of the rub see them shine see them possessed with truth! With purpose! With Oneida zeal!"

Braun steps back on the stagecoach takes a seat lets his
pard'ner handle this setup
(*sweating, nervous accomplished, brews a pot o' joe in a
sideways French press*)
(*sips it slow, thoughtfully*)
(*Let's it cool*)
(*drops a sugar cube by his feet*)
(*crunched to a billion glittering dreams*)

"A hand for my partner Braun here, he's the reeeee-*e-eeeeal* talker, right ladies and har har *geeeeerms,* Ah can never seem to shut him up. Now if you don't mind I got a story for ya. A story my daddy dun taught this ole cowboy heel—a'fore we git to this product, this here miracle product I got on display behind me, I feel I got to git to know ya, I can't jus' be giving this here this (big winding arm cartwheel motion fireworks flashing gesture) miraculous serum awaa-a-ay, so we're gonna shoot the shit, hey? Hit the breeze! ha har harp—now there's this fella, right, a real regerlar fella, he's gone down the pet store see? Wants a lil ole parrot to perch on his shoulder, so he inquires, ya? they got some displayed out at the front window, Eh? He wants one of those talkie parrots and he picks one out all green and red feathered, pays the faceless face at the register, lugs birdie home sets up the cage, sets it right up in the most central part of the living room and the bird is sitting there in his cage all set up and git this—no words—fella is waiting, conversing—this here lil' birdie got nothing to say! You believe that?"

Ken stares down the crowd, eye the sucker there there no-no-ah there. you. are! He clicks in his throat victoriously— "so nachurly the man takes the bird back to the pet store, 'this here talking parrot, ain't said not one god damn thing' well says the cashier, takin' this all in stride, you try buying him a wheel to run in? He runs in the wheel he's happy he maybe talk, no? Yeah the man says, that makes sense and he buys the wheel takes the parrot home, it's running in the wheel, running running but again says nothing. Next day, bright and early, our boy is back down at the pet store, and the cashier asks, 'you get him one of those mirrors you know? He runs in the wheel looks at hisself in the mirror starts talking, eh?' Nachurly our man buys the mirror, he'd already invested in cage and wheel no reason to stop now, takes it home, parrot is running in the wheel, looking at itself in the mirror, still nothing, not a damn word. Next day, the pet store again, he goes, 'look I got him the wheel, I got him the mirror, this bird ain't talked once, what're you trying to sell me, huh? You think I'm some kinda sucker?'

'Rest assured sir, I would never think such a thing,' he's assured by that same cashier, one offered the wheel n' mirror, one that sold the dang bird, 'this here bird talked all the time up until you purchased him. You get him a rope to hang on?" Yeah, he got him the rope too, and he's runnin' in the wheel, lookin' hisself up n' down in the mirror, hanging every which way on the rope, and ya know what?"

"What?!" the crowd hollered, "he ain't singed a'gin?!"

"Naw, ha *ha*, naw, catching on pretty good, now we're talkin'!" Kenneth replied, "Here we are the next morning, our man comes downstairs low on sleep, stress levels a'risin' been calling out sick from work for days, and there's the bird laying splayed out on the newspaper carpet at the bottom of the cage, you believe it as I'm right here talkin' to you, dead as a door nail. Dead. As. A. Doornail. D. E. A. D. So angrily he rushes off again to terrorize that same sorry cashier. 'Look here now!' he bellows, 'Ya sold me a faulty bird, and to top it off he never did talk once!' 'You sure? Not once not at all? Ever?' The cashier asks probing. Man thinks, drilling his slow witted brain creaking. 'Well, ya know,' he says, 'Last night, uh, last night, maybe, maybe I heard something, some kinda low raspy voice...sounded like, sounded like it was saying...'*fooooooood....fooooooooooo-oooood...*"

"See see! Har har har har"—Audience laughing now, sucker every minute every god damn minute. Braun sifting through the crowd lifting stories shifting pockets hands in coat overalls dusty Mississippi hands brushed against the nearest wallets pocketbags coat pockets bindle stick.

And before you know it caravan is out moving to the next snake juice oil tonic next sundown town...dust ahead dust clouds behind...loaded to the brim with stories of another time another town another space-mind-field-chime. Wasted.

"You catch a glimpse of 'em?" Ken peeks over at Braun the crowds a big dispersing cloud system dust field moving across the Midwest.

"Naw, no how. He'll show tho," Truthfully neither has seen the man's face, the biggest quietest secretist runner of illegal and interdimensional stolen goods on the 3D American tercentennial space.

"Before the cops?"

"Don't take my word for it. Bullets for clock strike twelve."

"We need that part or this baby won't go."

"How much cash we pull on this job?"

"Same as all the others."

"Ah, then none."

"These stories'll only power this machine for whatever-time, we'll never cross the mountain on Kansas car trouble cattle tipping waiter waitress tipping western diner living time, we need juice man, serious story juice to run this rig! You know the part! Best we've been doing is four miles a day!" Braun mouths with Ken's voice heard through the fracture of the essential ear.

"Better than hitchin' walking talkin' man I'm tired."

"You saying you thinking we don't need that part?"

"'Course ah ain't no man ah man ah shit, Braun," Ken chuckles let me have some fun before those cruisers descend, "Speak of the light and the fool."

"We been narced."

"Yaw *sheet*."

[*Cruisers are cop cars are baton beaters are sycophant-seeking gun-totting self-protecting warriors of the established monetary order rushing forward blue-red-blue-red-indigo-blood-indigo-blood-death whirl—*]

"Ah, shit man you mean, you mean I mean, I told ya that last town was too much! If we can't rustle out ol' Ronny we're gonna be punched sooner than later!" Braun laments, "Now we gotta shake the fuzz with the sunroof down. You're like that green man, that outlawed fiend."

"Robin hood?"

"Ack Suess' Grinch maybe I mean, who knew?"

"Fuck that a cat a devil a whore is nipping at my sole worn shoes, I got now-time, brother, no-time..." Ken laughs into the wind spin the colors playing ringing on his wine bottle jade kaleidoscopic goo, the squad cars those SWAT painted cars smashing crashing rushing forward guns blazing ho ho ho collateral damage be damned. See the warning label, sometime it's preferred.

"Hell man, now we got pork belly pinky pig Armageddon on our hands..."

Ken turns into the flashing lights, trip rotates colors like a ceiling fan with focus on one blade, both Rodman's reach into jacket pockets now, pens sunglasses gloves no guns just letters words there there the pickled pen is mightier than those outlandish tv antenna swords, you're just watching all day and night never turn that dial off technological story-time passive slaves.

"Gonna have to turn this ol' brute buick loose my fine friend, you know this baby has been towed at least through three states stolen..." Braun.

"Ah it's not quite ready to break the landscape wall." Ken.

The cops cattle crops closing in gearing through fields throwing fences up locking signs of private property warnings down. Cornfield down. Barbed wire down.

"Yo, this is some serious shit," Braun opines.

Both our boys laugh; they've seen worse where they've come from on the opposite side of the omni-verse at the sunrise omega beam big bang rise of the bleed. Race is on nonetheless.

Some vision on the horizon some singular ghost oh well—

Let's get this car chase, media darling blitz on the road for fuck crying shuck's sake.

They push the old clunker into the alley.

Pocket the snake juice catch.

Get your ass to mars.

Red light blue light revolving swinging by, the boys duck alleyway to alleyway making a beeline beez balm for old skid row dreams red carpets fine dining 5c hot dog sans casing bun mustard (katsup don't you dare).

Ken scales the cyclone fence between avenue A & B, reaches down hoists Braun up, they tumble in a laundry basket bundle on the opposite side face down in a rain puddle forgotten since last Tuesday afternoon. The splash throws an inky blue water—lands at the feet of torn old leather shoes, the smoking bum with the five o clock shadow.

He grunts. Exhales thick smoke into the atmospheric lung.

Glances—eyes first followed by head—sees the tweed damp bruised figures before him, shifts his seat the seer suit *fhhh fhhh fhhhhhing* on the metal trash can lid lets out an audible *haaaarh,* lets slip his hand when his vision focuses into view, the four arms waving gladly happily throwing rainbows of lethal stagnant sparks, there's a large hock of mucous caught at this very moment in his lungs forcing a dramatic and atom-bombic loud swallow only he can hear clanging, no sudden moves and maybe these two tweed assassins aren't here for me like a rabid dog just nice hobos nice hoboes maybe they don't recognize me man the fuzz man the man man the guns man the lam man the cheese maybe they won't recognize me as I go, still like stone like stone in the wind not creaking but his pupils give him away they vibrate at the criminal frequency the black market misery the back room romance of the dark street corner man con man machine man anything you need man junkyard vulture, but I'll just ignore them and they'll pass right by I'm sure and the cops, they'll leave me alone too they gotta there's nothing incriminating standing in an alley way waiting on a score freeze up like a deer in the yellow ringed enlarged headlight of time—

"Oh, fuck," he takes off running, cigarette and coat tails flying. *Fphlap sssss puff puff piss.* Described here in lanky terms as a ragged gazelle on yellow powder dreams.

"The Dealer!" Braun shouts, "It's gotta be him!"

"GRAGH!" Ken echoes, an echo of an echo that originates from a different sound. Braun shakes his head at the discordant *gragh gragh gragh gragh.*

"Doesn't sound anything like me," He shrugs, Ken is off and listening in the past knowing the game is on the loose and down. He's running for that trader man long thin legs eaten by opium hustling and sweating just out of his reach, head flashing alley to alley to turn signal duck over duck under hope the next dead end isn't until he's safely home. Ken touches his nose lightly. C'mon c'mon c'mon man I ain't gonna bite and we can't keep this up all day.

They're one two three running along the table tops of skid row outdoor cafes, climbing under the garbage trucks filled to brim with landfill waste, sweat pouring from every fiber of 3rd dimensional space. The prey the predator the muse.

Finally on alley way cut a brick walled dungeon.

Heels screech to stop and old man four floors above holds his ears jumps to his feet rushes to the window watches for the accident scene. Just three fucking bums. Over the siren yells screaming from miles away he yells—"You bums don't get outta here and get a job I'mma call the coppers I swear!"

Ronald is panting hands on hips.

"Now see…"

Now see here this is how it goes.

We phoned ahead see. For a part. For our four wheel cart.

We've got everything all set.

"So why chase me, man?" Ronald wondered.

"You ran."

"Oh."

He tears the concrete from the street floor, a solid illicit bunker underground, he sells opium uranium and anything under heaven with dead fingers, pockets the overhead.

"I'm fucked if the cops find me, Oh Esmeralda," talking to self, Braun and Ken watch on, throwing caution and piles of machinery in a pile on ground, "Christ just go through it will ya I swear to ol java I'll be hanged if'n they find me and you brought every pig from here to Omaha Neebraska here wit'cha. I'm assuming those sirens is for youse?"

The boys nod as children in the porch light of night.

"Hey, man sorry if it's too much…"

"We got a tip we'd could procure a transdimensionallocatorflipnswitchcarenginereplacement from ya?"

"True or no."

"True enough. I try not to carry these kinda things anymore."

Braun peels the first layer skin of his left hand and throws it on the ground, "Collateral."

Ronald jumping back, "fucking Christ in hell what the shit man! Looks like a snake hand! Why! Jeebus!"

Ken makes those few discerning looks, "Well if you're not happy I could brew up something…"

"Something like cash?"

Another hand layer of skin this time Ken's lands next to the first.

"What the fuck?"

"Take it or leave it."

"Who's there!" comes the autoreactive authoritative old blue growl from the search light just beamed down. The spiked caps, the sinister agenda. We have this alley surrounded. More wheels pouring in and certainly like toy pistols our guns our guns our guns.

"Oh, just take it," Ronald moans tossing the small fallopian thing to the boys before climbing into the chamber and locking it tight. Now get this no evidence only street remains.

"Time to scale those fire escape vines!" Ken yells levitating to the first rung.

"Ya just jumped you buffon," Braun taunts unbelieving pulling the ladder to the ground behind him rising up to the roof the tin heads of the man visible and shirking below past the window where the old man is yelling they're moving to the roof to the roof to the roof! GO GTFO GO GO GO the cop takes aim and luger kicks back three holes in the old man's heart. That'll teach him to disturb the peace. The jack boots return to their cars. The further expedition continue. The great societal search.

Braun and Kenneth circle back to the wagon, stop for a tonic and gin, skip the bill leaving three perfect round pebbles and an old tin can sailor behind.

Installation.
Elation. Here goes. Back on track.
West on that only road.
Lonely.
Hey Hey.
What a guy. Ya.
The wind in their hair. Snapping
The prah-prah-
Prairie ahead. Rest stop Kansas and Rocky Mountain joy on
the otherside.
The high high golden plain.
They call him Ronald the Dealer
He sells uranium gunpowder lead and—

Transdimensionallocatorflipnswitchcarenginereplacements
when the shadows grow long when the shadows grow long
"Luckily we slipped him a five finger discount
for a little bit and all three," Braun laughs.
Ken bent to the wheel.
The town in the rear.
The sun making its way toward another dawn.
It's lights and miles to go from here.

What was that song about the west and the going
that you knew?
			You know the one without a time
for the words?

You're entering a another paragraph,
a paragraph meant not only to transition a scene
but to begin an entire new adventure.
A scene both startling and new.
Next stop, the following sentence!

That last sentence before the stage change made from last paragraph goo through the use of the enter collection collage of words set into specific order to form sign is code for hyperspacetimemydarlings that was is code too spelled out in spacebar storm hyper-space-time-my-darlings read like *Old Susannah* Stephen Foster ballad (an order or a past tense disorder a parenthetical nonsensical drawl) with a banjo in the back seat the bleary blur blue lights of freedom arch up and howl. They had one more phase to make, enough energy for two. Some skies open up other cries boo hoo my angel babe there's infinite stars in the sky and the city blots out all those not meant for you. Emptiness, purple skies, you must have to please get out THERE before you die die die di hi hi hy hyperspace time is time distorted to an assigned reality to string and music flow, they [B and K] drop out un-aged plop down back of interstate one day later like it was no days later like it was no-time, after all this goes, after this adjacent story juxtaposition is told, their trail, cold.

Disclaimer: what follows may be understood in linear time. Your time. The time it takes to read, if read all in one line, one take. Do not put this down or you'll blow this whole gosh darn thing. Take a breath, it's up to you. Begin.

There's stars shooting forth and breaks and screeching awful smells rubber burning rubber smells and those cars spin out on prairie route I-70 going through red sky Kansas City.

A child crouched down in the midst of drifting dirt, speed, concrete, pebbles, old paint chipped, and jagged like road glass, used to be yellow, pure blazing white, now asphalt burned and tire rouged. Fender bender for miles four mile long trail down and out on that road it's Sunday night in the periscope darkness of the mid-west circular light of the fishbowl view your only light SLAM a child staggered like the worst deer in the headlights of the world and pulling the wheel just in time you take out sixty or so feet of median think of those taxpayer dollars and what the damage on your knight's car is going to be HOLY SHIT HOLY HELL THIS KID BETTER BE OKAY BETTER NOT BE SPLAT ON THE GORY PAVEMENT OH HELL WHAT'LL I DO AH CHRIST IN HELL BOY OH CHRIST IN HELL FORGIVE ME.

And in the center of the westbound lanes of I-70 wouldn't you believe it was that kid, the kid from New York City, that kid from tv news and Oprah oppressive impressionable interviews, that devoured sad child, that little boygirl covered our boys tracks the first time, the girlboy with the prairie dog shoes, the innocent eyes, the close cropped hair, the jewel of the earth, the boy-girl, the never was and always was ambiguous androgynous selfhood, humanhood, angelhead, godfart, that nothing is and everything is accepted believer in our lofty dream, that all is all and ever was the same and never again, amidst the pile up of police vehicles she slept, undaunted, unmoved, unafraid.

The first bluejacket to venture from his car that same ol'boy who'd yelled out in our last paragraph, near fainted when he saw what they'd very nearly almost hit.

"Chupa-fucking-capra!" His co-worker screeched, conspiracy cryptozoological bent, drawing back, terror-strick'd, vehement in his assertion of a monster thing goat sucking thing in the night-night flashlight beam, he fired off a clip, reloaded, repeated the same sane ejaculation.

"Jesus H helluva-night christ, man," His partner reasoned, "What the hell is wrong with you, now, get a'hold of yourself and look again, look," held steady he shined his little black regulation standard issue flashlight, "that there's a little boy or or or girl or or maybe I don't know, a child even…. And well, jeez, you could see it wasn't my fault when the gun went off I…to defend myself,…first…the case…the case… if you don't mind radio in the chief of the police of police police and let him know our con men have escaped…."

Radio feedback loop—

"We got a situation. And a clean-up."

"Cover-up."

"Copy."

Enter: Our Post-Dimensional Villain

Oh, fuck, for fuck's own god arranged fuck sake here goes the very fabric of reality's scepter shattered one more time. The crack of blue light, blur lightning bend of space and bubble of time, like the window breathing, rising and falling, contracting, expanding, breaking this thin curtain, the wall of understanding.

Clear your mind, listen and you'll hear an almost inaudible sundering sizzle of air, of friction on swishing Whitman-like leaves of grass, tiny hairs on the tiny legs of spiders stiffen, sniff for a slight burning smell in the funereal air, minute sparks of reality gasp and implode, die out, dried, like the bubbling on Yellowstone ledges, like the sulfur smell of the damned.

"Lo, I have crossed the chaotic trenches of tyme, the thirteen descending re-ascending layered levels of Dante's misbegotten hells, frozen the river Styx in my wake, it awaits my return, longingly. I am insatiate. I am unmoved. I am annihilator of worlds, all living and un-living beings are subject to my every whim and desire."

This a booming scoundrel's voice, like the unnerving sound of doubt in your conscious head, with the effect of falling to your death in lucid dream, a sick soul turning lurching stomp, the grating of nails on slate rocks, the death that came to Sarnath, the twisted bells ringing bells, silver bells, worst lie best told, most horrid death previous to being born. Imagine this in the trumpeting voice of the vision of fallen angels, re-animated corpses digging out revelatory coffins of the tombstones of the wet, sod ground. Entropy of time. This is horror nigh unimaginable on the horizon, harbinger of famine, pestilence, and death death Death.

Hear its herald ring:

This here is true evil shit. This here is unstoppable madness.
This is here is form given torment. This is the marching
army of DOOM.
This is what has traversed space to find its innocent target.
This is death a thousand million billion trillion fold.

Only the death of all existence shall quench my thirst
Only the bodies of your champions dead
Only their heads upon the hill
Only their tweed suits dyed
Only them gone and bled
Only only only only
Oh run run flee
Oh oh oh
Oh oh
No
no

We are too late, this marching calamity is long overdue

They have had one thought for millennia since the biggest
bang—

Kenneth and Braun Rodman those jazz age pulp hero swine

DEAD oh dead oh defiled oh dead, *oh lost!* Not merely dead but ruined destroyed vanquished bested beaten undone tweed jackets upon the fire of history un-re-remembered

I can't I can't describe the bleed and the years it took and the time between dimensions and what it has done what it has done, what sacrifice to get here, to stop that which must be done, there shall be no ascension, no next phase, no next great epoch, the collective subconscious unconscious eye must remain fourth dimensionally blind—

"And I will see to that," His laconic acid spit reply.

It'll have to wait, you'll see soon at the when the oh no tho but bu- if only...ah, Confrontations...inevitable... writ in star across time in constellation dreams. First the hunt, the chase, the round-up, then good oh drag good good deadly deathly tomb-like goodbyes...

Only one being could command this chapter, could bring reader and writer alone to their knees to wondering what's under the bed, what hand awaits, what being with preying eyes stands concealed in the closets of our child memory. That very singular one name feared in all dimensions, only one absurd, mal-formed creation could command this death's head breed just crossed through, now taken and molded into three dimensional space, that body, grossly, hideously formed. Body in early stages defies description. Defies sight. Defies shape.

One name one surname one *nom de plume* one dreaded *nom de guerre* one abhorrent *nom de morte.*

That inter-dimensional, intra-galactic, mustache twirling, muah hah ha ha-ing, uncompromising, intractable, indomitable, resolute fiend, that demon walking a magmatic salted earth trek through the realm of men, that sick zombie of the nether realms, may be respectfully, terrifyingly addressed as Mister—

Valentine,

Valentine Green.

Ever been to Junction City? Yeah, me neither. Bah.

Two hours due west of Kansas City KS, Kansas City, MO—fictional third dimensional sister city of Central and Keystone cities, DCU—sitting low on the lowest grayest edge of the lowdown dragged out brown and green midland in all of grassy plains America sits the little flat drawn out town of Junction City. If you find yourself there, word of advice, avoid the scrap yards, they retrofit cars and drive them for another 150 year at 150 dollar salvage no tip pop if you got the owner's card that is, if not dock 50 bucks off that credit drop. At a little corner called 5th and East, by the decayed remains of a wholesale cattle market (still in operation), on the wrongly right side of the railroad tracks, themselves floated up on piles of round multi-form maroon rocks, hammered deep by rusted spikes, chattering, battered, whole take in scene likeness of an old photograph distilling on your screensaver desktop cover image computer screen, runs straight arrow of Alt. Bus. Rt. US-40, parallel to big brother combination US-40/I-70 Main Street zero point two miles south, making its own glorious road gray-cloud-heaven-speared-way through this little misplaced country town. Nothing exists as it does on Google Maps. Nothing is always ever the same. If you see something today, it's dilapidated and dated tomorrow. Everything is gray. Everything and everything is gray. Everything.

There ain't no
convention towns
out west
 like Pocatello
anymore—

Braun on the left.

Ken on the right.

Interesting bit about the car here.

They've been bamboozled hood winked smeared.
A Real Lemon, Ken mutters, a real sour ass lemon. Sputtering in the night. What looked as fog rising from the mount was the burning engine of a part won't work of the head gasket meal time melt of a sucker trading skin for bone. Time of death Sunday morning hail shower 2 am.

"Serves us right I guess."

"Esmeralda bury the boy," muttered Braun into his fingerless gloves blowing smoke turned gray.

"She'll watch him swing on the gallows fer sure, that boy used to be a right trusty fellow a couple dozen years ago," Ken caught the yellow glow of the sunflower tattoo, turned it back into the gray sky where sits the sun somewhere in the galaxy across even as before, below.

"Nothing in it for him—aye."

"Stops us going home."

"Why'd ya have to go an' offend his Esmeralda, mahn?" Braun pulled at the last nerve nose hair in his index thumb finger grip tug and sneeze and times that by three.

Ken stares out into the wisp of Wheat Sea, smiling, incredulous, innocent, "Me? I didn't say a single word to the man, honest."

"Maybe he just wants us to stay love America love the land love the brave and the fee free blood white lines and forget the trek west love the Middle East black tar feast best death marching beast. They see what they got and stack pipes across it ass to ass blowing black guts on the green rollin' scape hittin' all the highest cloud mountain marks. A murky copper color inedible soup."

"Cynical fuck, I think you offended his delicate sensibilities when you didn't pay'em."

"You may be right," Braun releases the hair to the wind, hurtles back east. Good bye songs goodbye old hat. Release.

Relapse. "I'd like to think he ain't never once plugged it in the try."

"Whuh?"

"The device!"

"I'd like to draw an apple the size of the sky."

"You're a right Johnny Appleseed fuck, my man!"

"If only we had a dinosaur like the one'd he'd ride."

"That was a dinosaur ranch not a dinosaur station."

"I think you might mean Stallion?"

"Best move our asses if ever we'll make it to town." Yeah yeah.

Reentry didn't go as clean as planned. They're backpack on back walking on beat up shoes toward town, thumbs in back straps humming along, car dun dun been broke down down left hackneyed and rusted in a roadside ditch by a orange painted be-dotted, turn-off-here-in-1,000-feet-ramp-is-closed detour sign. Sing a ditty son, sing one for the lonely road, empty road, trip's end seeming ends, literal roadblock, stuck in stop, symbolically defunct nowhere to go nowhere to go it in, sounds a little bit like this one—Rodman's switch lines, feed transitions, go toe-to-toe lyric-to-lyric, pome-for-pome for 'bout a two mile crawl, they're in step, pounding the Flint Hill bridge old browned out sorry sagging wail of a bridge on that lazy, sluggish, Smoky Hill river, dandelion sun painted 40 at its heart unfazed, gazing down, something in the cloudy rain heavy air, their sad voices, their give up voices, they're never going home, never gonna find it, never gonna know it, man oh man *"we only wanted to get out THERE a bit further, pioneer treks and lofty dreams,"* confessions hum in rhyme break the fourth wall of eventual time, sound like two down and out remarkable, indefatigable old friends, goes, this back and forth poem about ol' cannonball run single thread to the coast and back, road mavericks of the American cross country road, singing it to themselves, mostly, the boys bopped on, empty bellies, harmony, tired legs, heavy eyes, boundless hearts, all, the words of a pome from a poet barely known:

Just so you know
I haven't forgotten—
been lugging my bag and
banging my head on
down that dusty road
West, been out and
gone in Junction City, Kansas-
style on a Sunday
nowheres to go and no
car to go it in—been lost and
cold and wet on that
highway life at 4am in
the thickest tar black night
you could imagine—been high too,
digging everything all silent in
my wanderers head—thinking

and writing whatever hellish unprintable
mash I could envision,
been takin' down the days the hours
the minutes as the tires turn wear out rot
and angle—seen every God damn
God fearing thing—unconquerable,
unquestioned—rising out of the
gray American fog—
lost all my words trying to figure out
what it is
where it went

***

...and I'll beg there for mercy for me

Back by the alley with the secret hatch. By the secret hatch and the cowering Dealer. EXT. Dusk. TIME. Simultaneous to the previous paragraphs. All the sirens pulled away to cover up the body of some little girl. Little girl *obstructing* justice. Reporters already out digging dirt. Matching up her name. Murderer, un-american, terrorist jelly bean. Officers must be allowed to protect themselves. Deadly force is a necessary vice.

Ronald, who he is, lowers himself down the ladder, empty bottles jiggling on his belt like wind chimes out on ranches of before the tornado landfall. There's darkness mixed with shadow. Empty hollow void sound. Then a sultry, lustful voice out the dark, a clap of thunder. A single hanging light bulb some odd-watt clicks on, flickers, *mmhmms*. There's that outline in the cast, bubbling over, irresistible.

"And they took the part," she says, teasing the words out, tonguing them, releasing them gravid with perfumed saliva. Only the perfect outline speaks. No movement. What I can make out. Related. Her hair falls down in coils to her shoulders. No sign of clothes, fabric must be skin tight dress as at her crossed legs the lip of a dress cut up to thigh. Long slender arms, playing on unlit cigarette breaking the line in two. Perfect pressure curves down from shoulder to breast to slender stomach dramatic hip long long god satan fearing legs. She purrs like a snake in its den. Rattles.

You called him Ronald the Dealer. He sold Uranium, gunpowder and Lead. Now he's in trouble stranger, the more you read on, the more you dare to tread.

"Y-Y-Yes Esmeralda. I sold those boys the lemon, they shouldn't make it past Junction. Just like you told me I hadda do when we left texas together," He wrung his hands scratched his face at the supple outline of her flesh, the dark reveal.

"Then you've done very well darling. Please, sit down."

"Oh. Oh kay." He shakes down to chair opposite her, the light displays the flesh of her hand milk white red fire finger tips. Click click cli-ck ckak one two three four down the line the thumb rubs imperceptibly along the surface, almost. Ronald sweats. Pulls at his shirt, tugs at the collar choking his neck.

Abruptly she's on her feet, O Esmeralda, She walks slow and stands behind, leans down and whispers, O Esmeralda, whispers in Ronald's weakened ear.

"I'll bring you supper, sweetheart," and the air burns on his ear tearing flesh and hair and skin away, cartilage melting slowly. She called him sweetheart, he's glad he left home.

The stew appears before him, steaming meat and carrots peas and potato, the bread torn off by hand beside, one large spoon next to it. He digs in slowly, increasing intensity as his hunger rises with each bite, mumbling growling, he pulls at the flesh, the fibrous vegetable stock. Esmeralda massages his veiny neck, the failing features of a man drugged by crime lust and feast. She lowers the bib around his neck, pulling tightly to lock it in place.

"It's almost tonight," She whispers, "The shadows have grown long, long enough. It's my time to go."

"Erm," He chews quizzically, thinking of those long slender legs.

"Yes, Ronny," She says, "There's just no time left to wait. It has to be now," as her voice turns and boils and her hands and knuckles go red.

"Mmmmhmrow? Mwwrhy?" the bits from the supper dribble down his tired chin. Ronald felt at the barbs of his neck much like rope rather than straw, he looked up at his darling Esmeralda, as the rope pulled and noose lifted. He was pulled up toward the ceiling, and as he swung over the crowd of one, he noticed quite starkly, that there was no Esmeralda, Just a man in a darkening hat and cloak, a sly grin rose on his ghastly face, like a bowl of dead fucking stars. The last face you'll see before the curtain. Oh fuck off lord, fuck me.

"I'm sorry my dear Ronny," He lamented, "You'll never see heaven or home."

His eyes bulged and brain hemorrhaged, kicking thoughts and his life before his head, was there ever a beautiful Esmeralda, as the knife slipped from Valentine's coat.

It was carved from a cuttlefish bone and it cut through him eerily like butter throwing his guts into the bowl full of lead, he'd ingested all of the uranium collected, his half-life shadow grown long and slow on the floor.

And again Valentine lamented, tears streaming from his absent eyes, "Oh Ronny, my Ronald the Dealer, no, no darling, you'll never see Heaven or home."

You've now been to Junction City. Gotcha.
Double-crossed.

"Well traveler, looks like we've taken the guise of the american what'd'ya call it american mendicant vagabond tramp drifter beggar ho-ho hobo beat up beat soul, no money lord, and no what anyhow to get at it," Braun gulped as the river receded into the distance they'd been walking how many miles how many hours now the brown muck and slow chuck of the waters breaks to squat road signs and yes, I think it might be, a little diner cropped up, rising as the sun rises over the flat happy earth land, there it was would you believe it carved out of the past going back what say you, maybe fifty odd years as a guess. Letters of the sign unintelligible unimaginable beautiful smell of eggs and toast and diesel engine idle roar.

"Sure as sure we find a way," Ken, undeterred, reiterated to himself and his other self, listened, responded, and he repeated out loud, "This is only a-a-a what you would you call it, a very well and understandable my-nor set back a very little bump in the road to the Rockies and the slopping slumber west."

"Ah," Braun grunted in slow agreement, scratching his chin, "But you know they ain't gonna let us go off free to test this green and ragged land, they're gonna send some ghoul to drag us back a'fore we make it coast to coast."

"I felt it'd be a jinx to say," Ken shucking corn as he goes, planting the seeds of idea in a row to hoe to sow to sorrow to tears to water to grow where they may.

"That myster~y, that Myster~v, Valentine, that deadly edgy Mr. Valentine..."

"Green, Green, Green my Valentine Green," words shudder and stutter out, "you're right about that B m'boy," Ken motioned to diner oasis before them, little jutting building with the little red lit letters, little jutting sign, filled out on both sides, "let us eat and talk about what's about to befall us and what and how we're gonna plan, to get on our road our track our *adventurette,* our journey again."

"Hell," Braun intoned, a few choice words snuck in [indecipherable], slapping his tweed coat, his roaring writer's block belt, with deft hand, "I could go for some strong bitter brew..."

Coffee awaits the hands on the mugs and the lips and mouths that take it in, to work its chaos magic sigil chocolate colored bean reverie on the very any many fool enough to reach out to jittery gods of caffeine and thought and those that aren't afraid to wonder, to ask what's at the heart of man, be gone, by god, be gone, bygones, and huge hot gulps and yes, ma'am a refill would be right great and thank you another, no no nothing else for me, just this splendid cup, and hours later here's where we've come and the diner is alive, and the diner is tantamount to the landscape of the gray space that cuts across the beauty of the spreading green glory that is that sea to shining sea drive, and when you've done what can never be undone when you've made it you get it and here and now forever there is that moment on the west coast, pacific golden sun shining, that can never be regained, but can never be taken away, a moment of pure bliss, hand flung out from car window traveling south, hot California, wind blue sky blue sea eternity.

In the quiet pocket of the diner's booth Braun motions for another cup gods and politicians and arbitrary lines be damned, Ken nods at his thinking might as well, we'll be up all night anyway by the foot by the starving edge of our sunken auto-cross-time-and-space-mobile, and we've got no plan on how to pull this sinking ship out of scuttle oh uh-uh uh-oh.

* * *

...and then I was the jewel of her sin

Back by the car. Back by the lonely car at night. EXT: Night. Second night. Very many stars and the Milky Way rising o'er sober sobbing landscape, Rodman brothers at the diner since noon long ago taking in the 24 hour service, free refills, sausage biscuits gravy from scratch, coffee and coffee again and eggs piled on eggs piled on all day all night (how do you make scrambled eggs? why, you scramble them of course) Stacey's (name o' said diner) stays open to, for and because of, specifically, them 18-wheeled cowboy pilots making long drawn out drives into the packing crate expanse mile-by-mile night of the drifting groundhog working day of liars. TIME: Now. Car been left alone, a-ban-doned, just an old buick now, disguised, lost all that 4D space cutting sailing ship spaceship sex shape. Just old and beat up out of date, sans automatic windows, auto-lock doors, kelley blue book defunct defenestration, wouldn't fetch 10 damn dollars in this state, dilapidated rusted out busted state it's in.

Slowly, silently ominously, a car pulls up can't really make out the shape, like it's got no shape; hard to see, pick out on the assembly line. Grayed out windows. Grayed great outdoors. Gray camouflage on the gray fog of night. No driver. Back side back door opens. Boot steps out, confident, direct, and camera catches it from angle of ground, the kick and mushroom cloud spout of dirt by heavy black (expertly polished) shoes. Grinding turn of heel, background crescendo of car after car after car on two lane stretch, hums and hums and burns out west, over the lower plains to high plains to holy rocky gray golden hills topped with snow. This man, this horror thing beyond imagination and time is invisible to the malleable minds and vision of men, and good for them. This evil live evil cannot be unseen, undone.

Ahem. Ah-ha. Smiling jester's mouth under turned down slouch hat, finger runs electric gyroscopic sparks over brim of hat a million women and their men cum in vicinity and don't know why a thousand babies die, down brim of time this little act of defiance holds them in temporal time, just long enough to dilute the soul of it all and lost their chance of endless nirvana, the ghosts and phantoms that walk the earth, enchained forevermore. This smacks of villains, masks and hatred, absurd bounty hunting claims, the snarl and gnashing of finely worn teeth.

This terror is none other than that garish demagogue, Valentine Green.

He checks the empty seats and smiles. The torn lining, rotted leather. The rotted out engine the rusted exterior, this car has no wheels no suspension no hope. It is falling backward through time from which it came. A sinister smile. Means it all goes to plan. His prey have abandoned it to earlier decades, they're on foot with only one town, one diner, one train track trick for ungodly cloudy illimitable prairie miles.

Behind him, ignorant of the scene he's making, the assorted blue jack shoes of the federated police neighborhood suspicion unit Uni-ited States, covers up the evidence, planting a body six feet deep.

"Hrumph," he spit old time style into the mud, black spew and dark brown goo. He sidles up, chewing the fat, twirling a rainbow baton in his delicate long fingers.

The coppers jump. Away from the sprawled body of a little girl. In her hands alive, the life filled body of a small chipmunk, saved by innocent arms at the point of contact.

"I was going by the book," said the largest, "I swear."

"We just gotta make sure it can't be traced," said the second largest, there were eight of them there, meaning four squad cars radio video silent, set on protect the peace.

"You're more faceless than a interdimensional ghost of death," Valentine's hissy breath.

They turn noticing his visage, scream, claw, Valentine pulls the trigger on the rainbow cane a million colors all the same a million human eyes can't see even a ninth of what goes into it. They tear each other apart, bloody blue waves pocket the earth, postmarked tears, bitter memories, early defaults. The last left is the tallest.

Valentine takes two steps.

Reaches out a hand. Cups the lawman chin.

"I'm sorry I'm sorry I'm sorry, I didn't know," cries real awakened tears of mushroom realization. He doesn't wanna get caught. He'll quit, never do it again.

"I know, I know, my Son," Valentine says softly, nurturing-like, "but see, *you* did."

The face comes off like melting butter, like cream cheese left out in rain.

Valentine turns back to the cars raises his hand.

They
burn
go up
in
flame
they sink
into the fertile soil
to start again

"Well, child," He kneels down, touches lightly her sweated brow, the munk growls, "it's time to wake up."

And she chokes and cries and the chipmunk yowls with joy and she turns to the roaches much beneath her, gleefully coughs up death.

She's out on I-70 alone. Munk runs up her shirt shifts its weight.

The clouds move like they've got eyes.

She knows where she's going now, touched by god the devil and both.

Free to walk the forever gray line from east to west.

Free to continue her quest.

* * *

Now you're a repeat offender

"He's here and no time, I felt the shift before the stars," Braun gestures, snap of fork into ice cream and cherry/blueberry/strawberry/berry pie *a la mode*, "He's already found the car, I assume, worked it for clues, clued on we've found ourselves here."—Ken interjects, "We're getting predictable in our old un-age."—"All the worlds and all that dimensional splitting filament space and every galactic universal bounty hunter in the pulpy genre horror-verse knows we can't resist a good old fashioned no frills baked into the sepia images of history's great turning memory middle of everywhere home cooked food'll stick to your gooey ribs, diner."

"Ahem, yah, ah ha, ah-ha, you know," Ken with idea space growth around his crown, been beaten back into place by his up-teenth cup of coffee and stacks of golden amber western thick pancakes, syruped and slurped down, fork glistening amber waves of grain in hand, "It's time for the Rodman boy's latest con and greatest of them all, in one foul swoop we fix the car problem and clear our greatest hurdle, mister too devilish for words Valentine Green, hit the grassy maw of earth ahead of our leaning skulls and fabled bodies, haggard minds, it's time for the world renowned, multiversally famous gag..." He waves in halting motions for the check like they're moving out and they are, they've occupied one single table, two chairs full, two chairs empty, for days and days, and the waitress lil' red haired Mary Beth James Hutchinson jumps to a start, hurries over, with the plastic-y paper of economic uncertainty—with a note the checks on us—Ken undeterred, stone-faced stoicism, bangs on, "the greatest caper in the history of Braun and Kenneth Rodman's travelling inter-dimensional circus circuitous circumambient bazaar of perambulation..."

Braun jumps up hits the ceiling hits the floor, staggered legs, green corduroy pants faded now into strange orange rust dust colored sheen, calls it even even eve-en more evermore, fixes his gloves (still fingerless, still sore) spins and pounds the left side of the table with his right hand (begloved, ecstatic), coffee mug flips, aged off-white ceramic, same as any diner you ever been in, in any states you've ever found yourself hungry or lost or both and there he drinks the final gulpy gasps, alternated with copious amounts of H20, and reads the grinds at the inner ring of the mug like the tea leaves of ancient forgotten aeons with one hand no hand all hands hand's free no hands at all, free sight, fool's sight, takes the last lukewarm eternal sip down, gives one long side look at his space crashing brother—who chews the word purposefully, resolutely, once again twirling the flipped coin of the world in his hand—awaiting the word already spilling from both their tongues, rolled out from both their transmogrified minds, their chattering blue lipped teeth, bearded chins of make believe, and make no mistake, these are words you'll read on the next line on the next page on the headline chapter line bold face line that in Times New Roman 12 point Kesey's *Sailor Song* final master font monster myth cheat code con man super spy superhero ti-ti-tit-toot-titular line plan proclaims....!

the Boxcar Bop!:
A study of the historical significance of the railcar

Cotton candy sky yes lofty plains a mile high I swear it.

The yellow hull of the Union Pacific locomotive engine distorted by swath of boreal blue sashes, pink cracked hitches, purple molds of crosshatch western wisps. Red faded letters painted long ago 1970 refurbished retrofitted and converted to high-speed passenger tail, metallic frames spell true, memories of ghost towns drift past and smell of dust, static odor, sweet smell of musty lost sneezes. These rockets keep going. The rail cars pull along toward the mountains—what's beyond them? Nothing and no one knows—invisible in the cosmos, the great continental divide.

It's a skeleton crew working, nobody much crosses westering in trains anymore—planes overhead hit the coast in no time at all birth transcontinental transplant conmen in eastern suits, thick sunglasses, long animal skin coats; cars are wasted in garage after garage in driveway after driveway prepared to junk it two hour commute to work in bright morning 365 days in the year, then maybe a few off next year to take a weekend trip to the nearest water hole and if you're lucky dinner and a beach crash haul, can't drive over the monthly mileage limit on brand new sparkling champagne lease—there's too much business to do in the allotted life-time, too many online newspaper articles to read.

Small freight picks up in Denver. Midnight. Edge of town. Old section tenderloin where the bums still mope and frown without having to spend too many nights locked up upside down eating cream corn from the can sucking on horehound hard candies biting with rotted teeth. Follow the trashcan fires blue tarps, turn in the opposite direction of bourgeois disgusted averted faces. You'll see them. If only we could shame them into working harder and 'get a job, ya louts!' the latest cardboard couple says.

Horn blares cold in the light. Breaks hiss. Sssssssssssss. Sonorous clangor cacophony of brakemen track switches station whistle train horn. Right on time. Always on time. The Ghoul train of the Rockies. The Ghostly Mountaineer in the Night. The last train, last chance, til' morning.

While the locomotive pays no mind, no never mind, no obvious concern, runs this bitch into the—conductor—the name of Gulch, Victor Gulch—makes this run by the ever changing night all the same—going headlong into the—wears the uniform perfect, by the book, to the T—rushing into the stillness of the—blue hat, thick wool coat, ticket hole puncher tucked in holster, hangs from belt, polished stainless steel— barrel unknown into the—and though perplexed by the jerky pitch and sway of the engine, nevertheless leans out, face cut by the cold motive of the night, one arm elbow hooked around the metal bar by the door, other swinging out into snowy thinning air darkness, swinging up to cup thin mouth, thinner moustache—forging out into the—his baritone holler booms once in tranquil night, as the crash of horse power roars— fiery comets trace out in the—shakes ground, swells, hand over hat now, an all-too-late-second-call, the platform in the—last night of a book cover light miniature, receded, gone—distance; He repeats—

"Winter Park. Granby, Steamboat Springs, Elk Springs, DINOSAUR, EX-PRESS! First'a' stop outta state. JEN-SEN. Ewe-Taw. ALL ABOOOOOOARD!"

Skit to heels as the train pulls out jut to platform smack. That's how you adjust a freighter boys this canned heat world ain't lost complete.

Victor turns back into the interior as the wheels as the train as the cars slide by platform to open air to rocky air—step by step and 78 steps exactly later he pushes the door open to the engine room—Eddy up next to walk the aisles, the sleepy aisles to pick the tickets to pick the brains of the dream brain of the sleepy passengers on board—all in a night's work—There's only so few straight lines you can trek on the chugging beast at the top of the world. So he quick shakes Gulch's hand who ballerina like spins to his seat hat over face covering eyes to spend his usual nap between stops and he's snoring by the swing and close of the door.

Eddy is almost opposite middle of the road hasn't washed his pants in 8 months—wears the same pants thinks nobody notices and nobody does notice but he suspects they might so he's self-consciously apathetic, his shirt is caked in cat hair—two little ones fur babies at home—hat is rumbled and pulled tight over his head that might just be too large by an inch for the rest of his frame—clicks the clicker in hand to snap the tickets just cause he likes the feeling of it clicking in his hand and also the sound of the clicking in the feeling in his hand is something like the clicking of battery lid on the back of the remote control as it slides open snaps closed. Down the hallway employees only signs red lit hallway out into the passenger car and he thinks about his dinner in the brown bag in the locker in the back cab and if he should wait two or maybe 3 hours before he digs in when the door slide and the florescent bulbs of the pass car lit in his eyes something else and something he knew but was not ready for lived in light for the carry-on-ers of the world going from point east to point west when he goes in a line back and forth and what's the difference clack clack clack ticket please ticket where are you getting off where did you get on ok ok clack clack it's much better feeling in his hand without the paper of the ticket in between and he doesn't even notice the two men at the table in tattered tweeds when he skips over them and swiftly makes his way for the next car and those men not looking up to not let him know they've been passed too intent on the cards in their hand and the third man at the table whose ticket was clacked (not to mention the assembled mendicants of the earth who lounge about the car seemingly invisible to the pay to ride scam i.e. they'll come up and get name tag labels as we go) but Eddy held on and took the ticket with him by mistake (which he does every now and then stuffed in his pocket destroyed in the wash never found) but the third man is also not paying any mind for entirely different reasons having stolen his ticket from some poor sap sleeping in at the last station on a bench rolled out, and having done so regretfully but needlessly self-consciously laughs out loud but more so to himself and asks:

"Which way you fellas wanna deal this hand? Clockwise or what, yeah?"

"Wheeeel, mister...ah, Forshmak? How's about you cutting this hand for ol'Kenneth here and we proceed from there?" said Braun with a slight mischievous smile.

"Forshmak Toot, billionaire adventurer idiot magician genius, PRESIDENT," said the bum on the bench behind sipping rotgut five bottles down, his crooked busted up nose bulbous and red painted raw like his brown jacket lived in oil fetish for the soul his shirt barely hanging on to his shoulders his pants sold for the rotgut he will regrettably inevitably pass around, boys call him Slim God Moe and only God or some other equally omniscient character knows his real name cause sadly after these many years on the road and boxcar and tail he's plum forgotten what his mama called'em, too.

"Don't forget Shaman," Ken inserted directly in line. Forshmak, furrowed brow on his cards, refused to notice the chatter round his head, tho he smiled, you know he smiled, couldn't help it that he smiled. The room was his.

"Listen to the Asshole, the rule was your hat backward and you mouth clamped!" booming vocal clash from the bum Sawtooth Pudding in the jeff cap leaning on Moe's back tipping the wine up to the train car yarn, his eyes permanently closed in the saddest upside down red clown smile you'd think to see on gray Newark streets in the haze of summer cooking under six layers of coats pants fabric shopping cart wool cotton sheep and in response Mr Forshmak reached out and turned Ken's invisible hat—as he wasn't wearing any hat—backward, the bums quieting down either for the pantomime or the fear that the bottle was empty and they'd have to sneak in the dining car again—Moe thinking to himself 'where's that fucker Red, Packing Red with that canned heat he owes me where's that rat bastid with the goods? Fuck'all, I'm fucked. What're my kid's names again? Oh, Mary, Mary, I screwed up!' could be his wife's name but the seriousness of the game dug these emotions unwillingly out of the two old spectators. The combatants now consider they're considering they may have bitten off more than they could chew from a real ripe feller a real card shark kinda silent strange fella, Ken sliding a note to Braun as the action goes: "This guy plays Asshole for keeps." Consider this little note meaning they're fucked and Braun slides over to Ken and catcher's mit in front of flapping mouth face says loudly, "We're fucked. You specifically, more than me I think." Moe and Pudding shouting, 'Heard that! Heard that boy howdy! Heard that!'

Ken pursing his lips making out the drama game, cards out on the microscope desk of transparency flips the words out like this, "Look, I said Mr Toot here sure plays asshole for keeps."

"Sure does! Sure does boy howdy! Sure does!"

"What you got to say to that Mr….Toot?"

Let's run down the list real quick*:

red top hat (yeah this true, red with a black band tall tall hat)

pressed hard on black curls
thick rimmed thick lens glasses
eye patch over alternating eyes, depends on which is being
used to think
yellow sweater, easter egg color pastel palette no under
shirt, wool stretched out stained with various life choices,
criminal voices
khaki slacks out a century back,
loafers over silk socks,
rubs his lips between plum thumb fingers the bones shifting
in and out the skin like water snake jello jiggling,
he snorts snuffs puffs sneaks the dope
is ready to pounce and claim the next rule
the next and last and final game

Ed. Note: Remember this is not strictly prose. ~BKR

"Asshole is a game of sincere and severe concentration. My people the Toots have played it as legend foretold they would from the beginning to the end to the dawn to the dusk of time."

"Remember this is not strictly prose…" Braun.

"Right right you right." Ken

"Asshole's like poetry."

"Don't I know it," Seethed a voice from beyond a voice from a body standing behind their backs Ken and Braun and no player at the table looking up even Forshmak who faced this ambiguously, could you believe it, a tunnel an overpass rush of cloud at the exact right moment to cast a flash of ululating shadow on this obscured scarecrow-like shade but kept his eyes down he did to the deck, to his life, to his hand, to holding onto one and then the other in both, the voice continued without surprise at downcast eyes saying what was generally understood by the three non-lookers at the table to be what would logically be said next by the figure just beyond their peripheral sight as said, asking, more than demanding there was no going back or saying no no forgive us sir ma'am madam guy no, there's just no possible, asking him to go, "Got *room* from one more, eh?"

Kenneth, hrumpt hrump harp, heart pump pumpt pound parpt, "Why why why yes, my good man of course. Take a seat. Uh, ha ah. Take a seat. Pull up a chair. Take. A. Seat."

And now, now from three there are four. Asshole's the name of the game.

And the cards.

52.

In one hand.

Dealt.

Šest generacija budala u potrazi za zlatom lude;

a lazy translation

Moon rises over the hurtling train. The color and shape. Half leftover coffee stain. Diner table it glows from carved by a billion billion years of exploding creation steam. The track unseen. But that train. It rushes like mercury silver and glowing through the night of western Colorado, border, eastern Utah. Purple mountains around. Black paper giants against the sky. Majesty. The last car is filling up. Wheels about to hit top speed.

In shoves loud and bloody belligerent (knowing he's not brought enough wine) missing duo Packing Red and Microfiche Cain carrying not the promised hard stuff but sugar death red wine.

"Good-night Irene! Good-night I-rene! Iiii-Rene Good-NIGHT!"—singing eyes closed.

They kick swing bash that fucking train door.

They throw they arms out.

They wait for they other voices to join.

"I kiss (we kiss) you in (our) my dreams!"

There's a blackhole where they sound supposed to be.

Moe is shushing hiding in his roll up sleepy bag. Sawtooth Pudding is darning his socks, squinted eyes, eying that bottle between 'em ain't getting up.

They take a moment (you know Packing and Cain).

Finish they last few bars—weakly.

"There's some shit here going down here fuck hell man I ain't be the one sign up for this," Packing's not much for remembering how to whisper. But all his life (the two years he got left after the close of this story died out on the streets some say Pocatello some say Denver San Jose Pie New Mexico Some old town Colorado USA from exposure and drink tho not from the decay of his liver per se more like the breakdown of the body inside ya know) he'll remember the slow turnaround of that ambiguous face, that sneer cartoonial plague like face those sharp teeth otherworldly filed sharp what was it a nose? Like nothing was there and Jesus Christ were there eyes he'd say over the fire I'd stake it on my mother's soul there were no eyes you gotta believe the damndest scariest thing you'd ever seen, made me quit drinking for a-a-a- year I bet as he slicked his hair back egg yeller around the fire and the other bums laughing and handing him the bottle he gladly drank the last bottle he'd ever drink they'd find him in the morning hand thrown out pointing at the road he'd collapsed by like at a phantom ghost and they pushed him into the woods left him to rot cause who needs a dead bum and the cops'll require too much answer too much time and there's many more bottles and days to find poor sad sad dead Packing froze at the skeletal back hunched over the table the semblance of a card game he tore off his hat fidgeted with it between oil dark fingers few nails missing like his mother yelled at him at church for picking a quarter out the po' box he threw his eyes like a fireman dive onto the floor the grand authority of death had filled the room.

"Muh-muhmuhmuhmuhmuh"—Microfiche smacking his hand hard on the chest a thwak of mucous dislodged and flung its way to freedom jettisoned across the room and took leave out the only open crack in the too few windowed cabin—"my ahh ahpologies sur didn't know they boys had a game going in here, I'll uh we'll take our leave now if it please ya."

"It would please me *greatly*," The figure spoke, slowly, deliberately, menacingly, "If you boys would take a seat *along* with your friends over in the corner *there*. I'm sure you'll enjoy the game we have going here as much as they have been. Sportsmen you must be, *yes?*"

"Oh oh definitely mister!" Microfiche dropped down cross-legged on the floor. Rolling his eyes in the bottle *di jour* motioning for Red to get the fuck down before the bombs go off and the shrapnel cuts them to pieces. So they both become spectators of the scene. Hostages at the corral. Unwilling participants in the ga—get it. *Sneer.* You're advancing downward peering over the edge. Hey, no doubt, it's the bottom of the world.

And that's where it begins.

—Okay ye bums

Ken in his best board-game-rule-

reading-authoritative-(but ya know

soothing-understanding-slightly-

maligning-a-bit-condescening-but-

not-so-outwardly-so-as-to-be-

obvious-and-called-out-on-it)-

auctioneer-rattling-voice goes

—the name of the game is asshole, the turns will go left to right starting one single persona, see person, persona, the next warm blooded (I hope ha-ha) body left of the dealer, who at this time would be me

He motions first to Toot sitting to his left.

—Mr. President.

Then to Valentine.

—Vice President.

Now Braun. Chuckles to himself.

—Vice Asshole.

Rubs the lapels guarding his chest. Puffs out his beard.

—Asshole.

At this point history says he raised

an index finger the one on his right

hand. Well, my friend, sometimes

history lies. Years later Ken won't be

able to recall why he did it, being

right handed himself, curiously, and

running counter to the historical

argument, he raised the index on his

left.

—Here's how it's gonna play. A bit Verbose.

Points to Valentine and winks. No joke.

—Any card played beyond the first card (which my friends is the highest card played no matter what considering it is played on the void of card on table) however if an equal card is played, well then, we skip the next player going left. You may play one two three cards at a time or as impossible as it sounds four if you're the first to play. See here, Aces are thee highest *non-special card*, 3s are thee lowliest of the bunch. Each of you will be dealt 7 cards per hand, why? Because I chose the number. The last player to empty their hand will inherit all the cards in the pile and we'll deal again until the 52 *wink* are depleted.

—2s my lil biddies, are a special card, they clear the field and allow the allotter the chance to drop a card to start the round again. The cabinet positions are deciphered as such and I quoth, 'based on the order that players were able to play all their cards. First to finish is President next game, second is vice president, second-to-last is Vice-Asshole, and last is Asshole.' Dig, the Prez, we'll fast forward, may make any rule of their choosing to be followed in the next round, the asshole, as a living breathing asshole, must obey. As this is a drinking game first and fore-thee-most you must drink—

The bums cheer to that, gulping down the
red. Swill. Chill. Drink it warm.

—Ahem. You must drink, when you pass, when you get skipped, when a 2 is played, whenever someone ranking above you tells you to drink. Wooooooeeey—

"How gracious for you to explain the game, I didn't catch your name…?" Sssss-ed by Mr. Green.

"No I guess you didn't," Ken smiled.

"How about, as a gesture of my gratitude, I supply the drink," from under the table Valentine produced a black hole void like bottle sucking light from the room the lanterns flicker the voices inverted, the chandelier appeared in Victorian style became a gas lantern burped and blotted out, the lights lit up again and the bottle heavy nearly tearing through cellulose on the table surface alighted staggered shifted held almost impossible like perfect form, on the label the sneering smile that hovered above it. The terrifying visage of Valentine Green. Graviton Absinthe an Old Family Recipe from the Oldest World Oldest Europa Moon of Jupitar along the black black maybe violet if you stared enough and hadn't lost your sight label read, *"Entropy Awaits."*

"How generous of you mister…?" Braun leans as far 'cross the table as the table dares to go, "I don't think I caught your name?"

"No," Valentine, flatly as the cork pops and sinks into the licorice mix, wafts of toxic chemical smells, black hole void smells, overtake the cabin air, twist and snap the sinuses of the living, Moe vomits red ruby guts into the corner spittoon, hacking, cracking, coughing, heaving, wipes his mouth with greasy coat sleeve, chases the bile in his mouth with a pop of the good stuff, that old dead man's wine, "No I suppose I forgot to mention it."

"Fair enough," Forshmak cackles, dropping 3 Aces.

"Bit early for that!" Packing laughs and laughs.

"My daddy told me I'd be president someday," He replies jovially, "and I intend to see it through," winks all around. Valentine produces from his bag four miniature gray skulls, places an elaborate absinthe silver spoon over each, in front of Braun, what appears to be a hawk, Ken, the soaring shape of America's winged Eagle, coughing he places in front of Toot the likeness of a warthog, and for himself a skull to match the bones in his long fingered hands, for each a bluish sugar cube radiant in the flickering candles, iridescent, in low light, over each a steady heavy viscous think pour glow yourself in the dark metallic blue that becomes like milk as it breaks and breaks down the cube, it's all filled to the brim, and after like pope pius XII he raises the drink up, his arms brush the ceiling scape, the cups hissing, bubbling, boiling.

"A toast," He attempts to smile cheerfully, dulled by the rows and rows of sharp pointed teeth, the brim of hat over his lack of eyes, "to new and old friends, yet to be born, and those long *dead*," he says, putting the cup to his lips. In turn each member does the same. Braun wince, Ken happily gulps, Forshmak tears in his eyes, lump in his throat—

"Well, I'll be damned! You boys know how to party, cheers!" He replies, follows up with a second sip.

Whispering back and forth *psss psss psss psss* waiting for the cats to appear Ken in Braun Rodman's ear, "I don't think he's picking up on the *significant* undertones of this encounter."

"Yeah, he's never gonna get my vote for president that way."

"I think he means to win the game, not actually run for third dimensional imperial policy."

"Polity?"

"Politely."

"Not likely."

"Rightly."

One last whisper, "Oh, ya know Ken, that makes sense."

The boys look up to the smiling, attentive (if not grotesquely pale) face of Mr. Green. He snaps down his last card never looking away, "I guess the winner of the first hand is me."

Ken and Braun still hold 11 between. Forshmak matches the number set and skips, cut throat mean.

"I'll take vice-pres, I guess," He glances around, "For now anyways."

And that's how it went, four hands in each time the same finish:

VG Drink drink FT drink Drink drink drink

KR—drink—drink drink—drink drink drink—burp—head teetering drink—BR

(They alternated vice-asshole and asshole building up a mountain of skipped turns and innumerable mounds of cards.)

"Now that I've won four hands," Green sneered and Braun

uh dealered… "I will make a new rule…for each card played, I'll ask a question so we can get to know each other as we play. We must be truthful in all respects, in that way, as president, I will hold myself to task. I will answer any and all question I ask."

"If'it's'gah'ana'thin'ta'd'wit'his'l'qur'ou'bin'peddlin'm'all' ears…" Ken slurred face in his cup breathing in the sordid fumes.

"What brings you boys here?"

Glances all around.

Ah, mean it.

"On my up'ta Pocatello to the convention, me," Pipes up Packing swilling and swirling in his rum dumb reverie, "Bout time I saw the ole boys again. You know I yous'ta live up this way with mother and the kid, but ya know that was a long…"

Green hand raised, limp wrist, "*Kindly, sirrrrrrr* (drawls out the ur like a growl low and like a dog whistle like a dog growl so's the train vibrates to scale, "I wasn't talking to you."

"Road trip, see," Boys answer together.

"As for me, the great Forshmak Toot, doubtless you've heard of me, and my traveling menagerie my traveling band of which I am the tireless lead the tireless beloved of many out here on the great plains, I'm talking about my circus, I mean of course, I believe many here have lent their hand once or twice, if I'm not mistaken, no no and I never am that's me the fantastic formidable Forshmak Toot, of *Toot's Totally Tortuous Terrific Internationale World Wide Phenomenon Circus of the Stars, LLC, Restricted and Trademarked.*"

"Thought I recognized that shyster!" Sawtooth jumps to his feet, bearing fists, "Bastard squeezed me out of all my pay left me destitute outside of lake Lanier along the side of destitute way Georgia!"

"The pun couldn't go to waste, very sorry my good man!" Toot smiled, edging on his seat closer to the Rodman boys.

"I'll knock yer teeth out!" Sawtooth launches himself freezing in mid swing mid air mid leap mid anger mid dive reversed backward and takes his seat scowl turns to lobotomized grin drool trickles down the side of his unshaved chin.

Valentine turns slowly away like his face turns then the time turns then his face turns again from the shadow blink and you'll miss it but it'll be rigged up into your subconscious mind brrrrr.

"Any of these other men make your acquaintance, Mr. Toot?"

"Erp."

"Nope. Nope, not that I know."

An icy finger on his shoulder, Green's teeth lean in to ear, "Make sure you supply fair wages next time."

Here the cards go again, here the Rodman contingent goes down hard.

"Road Trip you say?"

"Hey, Brother, you never answered the last one!"

"Silly me, I am also on the road. Interesting that you are on a road trip without a car. What happened to it?"

"Oh, that old bird. Broke down on us. Outside what? Where was it, Ken?"

"O'dat'tow'ya'Junt'sion'city,   just'n'city'KANS'as. If'n'm'not'mist'ken."

"Never owned a car mind you," Toot talking to himself, "It was, Oh, I'd say, spring, summer, winter? could'a been spring that year, that, yeeeeeeeeeear what was it, had to be, what? 1984-1985 spring-summer, I bought my caboose, that's what I called the old doll, CA-Boose! Big ass, loud engine, sold it to start this here circus, well, honest, I'm traveling ahead, gonna meet it in Cal-i-forn-i-a, be there a few days before the convey rolls in, man that was a grand old car, I miss, but, I got all this now," Touches lightly the brim of flaming red hat, "wouldn't trade it back…"

"Yes, *that*, is all fine and good," Valentine answers restrained. Strained. Teeth grindingly cordial, "We're all very, very *happy* for you."

"You said it my friend, you said it, had to be winter now I'm thinking about it, near the end of fall, I had a jacket on as I recall, maybe, though, maybe, I'm wrong, it was most certainly around 1985, I'd bet my circus on it. The circus I traded that very car for…"

The Rodman's huddle up, serious, "Ken, what's he talking about?"

"I dunno who to fear more man."

"I'm gonna go with Toot."

The next hand, shit, it goes from bad to bad.

"I passed an abandoned car in Junction City, without a doubt I remember it," Valentine leans in.

"Swear they got some secret weapon there," Braun undeterred.

"W'even'foun'som'tags'signs'rom'a'group'hadda'breakdo wn'jus'like'us'ou'bele'hat?"

"Oh, I do. However unlikely."

"Junk yard is about thirty, thirty-eight football fields wide."

"Interesting. So, your reasoning for the trip, then? I'd be really interested to know. I'll let you in on mine," the cards burning up like photos in his hands, the table sneering a terrified grin, for the first time the teeth sucking like suction begin to unwind to open, "I am here to catch two criminals, two worthless, rambling, pariahs, and I think, I think, I am *very very close…*"

A gun shot **BLAM!** Another **BLAM!** Straight into the ceiling.

Two figures hold on to the rail, the car door swinging open to that eastern Utah air dusters blowing in the desert scare a six shooter apiece.

"Heard somebody ordered two criminals, two worthless, rambling, pariahs? Well here they are for ya!" The figures bound in, overtake the floor locked bums. Point guns to their heads, the one, the other to the table sitting four men. A short, beat man in a brown duster, blue jeans, red scarf, bald head, scowling, mean, jagged beat up beak of a nose, his partner, beautiful red head, red duster, blue jeans, yellow scarf, silver plated Winchester in gold nail polished hands.

"As you can already guess," She says in a sly fox's voice, "This here's a stick up, train robbery, and we, your humble servants, are the greater-than-bonnie-and-clyde, the infamously famous duo of death and disgrace, Tesse Slake and Gummy Joe Miles wanted in all 50 states of despair and matter in all its forms. Now, if you'd kindly place all your least valuable belongings in this bag, you can keep the beating blood bag filled most important things to you, alive."

"Oh, for fuck's *sake*," Valentine Green mutters under his breath dropping his penultimate presidential winning last card, un-holstering the pistol in his left jacket pocket, dropping his dispassionate disguise, dropping his right shoulder, dropping his finger to the trigger, dropping his sights on two warm frenzied train robbing bodies.

"Hey funny man!" From the lips of the fox.

"Hands in the air and eyes where we can see them," Squawk of the Gummy.

"Easy!"

Gun hand shakes.

Pupils dilate.

Forehead sweat.

Fear makes.

Intractable decisions.

—Let's not have this turn into a blood bath. *Braun reaches into his lapel pin hand sinking into the voidish space the after hours speakeasy wallet space*

Gummy trains (ha) his gun on Braun. Woah!

 THE BOXCAR BOP

—Hey now, I was only trying to make friends! *His hands up* I only meant to throw some gold coins down partner…

Valentine quick draw pulls his gun up. Woah!

Woah woah woah waogh waohf woah

Gummy on Braun. Tesse on Green. Green on Gummy. Stand-off.

Relax!

—Wuz'zis'll'aboot? *Ken clumsily adds* les'll'giyt'ah'drink'eh?

"Too many of you bums are talkin'!" Tesse shouts, "Now, everything you own or else."

Moe starts stumbling toward the bag, motions toward it with big cigar fingers.

"You want I should just crawl in or what? Hauh! Only thing I owns is meself!"

Gummy convulses guffaws, splits, sides over, hands on knees, high pitched laughter, eyes tearing, stomach seizing, Tesse joins in dropping pistol to one side, laughter quickly like a wave picks up shakes Moe, Gummy kisses his oily scalp, Puddin', Packing and Microfiche line up in turn, shouts, last of the bums slapping his knee joyously they rush up patting Tesse and Bird on the back hugs all around, a reunion on the bum car in the bummiest western most moving train in all the track laid United States.

Ken leans over to Valentine, steaming red over grim white skin, "Eye'thint'them'boys'knows'each'odder'seas…ha ha ha ha."

Valentine only shakes his head and takes his pistol back home, where they rest.

"Nice piece, mister," Toot winks.

Valentine can only bristle, heave, grind his needle-like teeth.

From out of the bag, tumbles the treasure Gummy and Slakes, lifted from the meal car the restaurant car, the petty thief car, the fill your stomach car. We got the list but first:

Breakdown the weakest wooden bench
Put your back into it
Tear out the useless padding meant for your ass
It won't burn the way ya need it
stick it in your shoes
Strip the wood lining off the old door frame
Snap it over your knee
Kick at the weakest point
Let the cellulose snap

—shit these bums work fast! *Braun forgetting a card game was on*

drop it in piles
Separated by size
Build the first circle with wood chips
Cross hatch the medium twigs
Tesse brought a slice of flint
Microfiche flips out his rusted knife

A spark
A'twirlin' bit of smoke
A growing flame

Gummy leans in to blow
Moe grips his underwear pulls tight but the band of fetid undergarment breaks
Gummy just laughs and his laugh brings up the flame

And a face full'a soot

Now that grocery list:

1. rounded and packed in Tilapia fishcakes (mostly
breading)
2. slices of Black Swan (fresh caught over 3 months ago and
salted down)
3. a dozen or so free-range eggs (probably more like eight,
carton's missing)
4. half loaf of sourdough bread (stale and becoming
progressively staler)
5. coffee grinds (enough to go around and a second cup
served black no cream no whipped
                    cream no frosting no sugar no liquid
fructose no minimum of bitter solid grinds
                to chew)

    on deformed
dented
        sheets of tin
                    held over flame
        slice of salted black swan
dance
    curl   on rising fat
        grease
drips
    crackles
            smokes on burning wood
charred in fire
        in the oil remains
    drop the eggs in
                    sizzle the fish cakes
fry
    the scent of bread
beside in old
        1930 aluminum can
    Coffee boils
            savor
                that bit of heaven

before the poor meal
                  poor mouths
      poor hands
         poor past
              poor future
       poor come back to earth

Bums send the food around, split it up, dropdown around the fire. Gummy climbs down from the ceiling after knocking a hole in the roof for the smoke to peek through. They dine.

Back to the game.

"Where were we…" Green purrs. Forshmak slides his cards starts the round over again.

"'Could'a'swore'Mista'Toot'ere'place'a'differn't'card'fore'ta'b ums'came'in?" Ken slobbers into Green's hands, "innerrestin'cooticals'sir'. ovecraftin'sir'. macabr'sir.

'n'need'a'ome'work'sir…"

"Doesn't matter, I'm sure Forshmak would never cheat us, *yes?*" Green's neck strains toward his unwanted opponent.

"Oh, a beautiful girl. I dreamt all night of one," Microfiche chowing on his swan.

"Me? Never. Everyone knows. This red hat means anything but untrustworthy. Psk" Toot winks and clicks his tongue.

"If only there be one abouts. Eh?" Checking the room.

"A joy," Valentine gargles, playing three cards, skipping Ken, hand goes to Braun.

He passes, there's nothing in his hand he cares to let go, "You're running circles around me and my associate here," Glugging a glag of 'sinthe doom, "Agh! Stwong suff!"

"You better look the other way round," Tesse retorts.

"Aww c'mon baby."

"Eh, shuddap," Moe.

"Looks like this game is winding out of control for us."

"Na'ooking'ood'jis'chis."

"I say! I saw a beautiful girl and ah dreamed of one."

"Lay off callin' me baby, bum."

"Ken, you don't look so good, stop taking ten minute sips, yeah?"

"Eat yer dang food."

"Be'r'fine. Bare'y'stan'up."

"Ah, I'll eat it but I swear I dreamt it."

"Fuck off," Tesse hair in plate.

"Whatever in this brew brother, it's weighing me down. I can barely stand."

"Honey," Microfiche leers, "baby."

"Said leave off," Tesse stands.

Over the rising sound of denture and gums smacking the game goes on. Sure enough the outcome is the same. Green leans back over devastated cardboard fields, kings, queens, jacks 10s all lame. Microfiche reclines back on the floor eyes digging holes.

"Hey! This yeller aeg is raw!" Microfiche shouting throws his sandwich into the pyre.

My question this time— *Victorious Green*

"What of it?"

My quest— *can't get a word in*

"What of it! I demand a new one!"

My question is on the subject of your— *almost there*

"This eggs only good to slick back yer hair," Microfiche reaches for a thigh…

YOUR NAMES— *Yuggoth screams and eldritch frustrations*

BLAM! Microfiche gets a bullet to the gut instead.

Braun casually turns to face the scene, without looking responds, "Now, Mr. Valentine is this really the time to be asking on about our names, there's a man dying over there."

"Mr… *Valen…*" Green begins, but the door to the cabin swings open, an old leather face, beard like steel wool, eyes gray as rainy skies, a long deep scar nicking the bone travels like the mississipi down his ill-gotten face, body standing six foot four six foot five, long arms, beaten overcoat, stained worn jeans, high cowboy boots, under heavy cowboy hat gotta be what 20-25 gallons, dunno, don't have a chart, he clanks in, spurs snapping firecrackers on the car floor, only wood bums ain't tore up. What's the bet on this being the law or the medical staff or neither or both. "Came here," voice growls sounds like a cat food can opening in can opener thrust inside a dishwashing machine, "Came here cause'n I smelled that black swan," He laughs like a lawnmower blade, doffs his cap, takes a seat, "My friends call me Scarface, you can call me Scarface Jock. Now pass me a mother fucking plate."

Microfiche groans holding his stomach his sandwich his guts his black swan his blood his eggs his life his supper his pain his hunger his tears. The bums around him. Tesse gets a quick kick in. They all notice the body relaxing guzzling the coffee down, blood running all over his snake skin boots. He glances up, hunk of swan out his broken black teeth, "Woo-ee Lookin' like this boy here's been shot, eh? Or you on the lean, son? You look positively euphoric about ready to pass out!"

"I've been shot…" Microfiche muttered to himself.

"Deserved it," Tesse spat in his face placing pressure on the wound with a gray bandana.

Ken is sprawled out on the table, bubbles of thought clogging the hole in the roof smoking everyone out. Valentine looks crosswise at Braun, chuckles, glances down at the cards, motions with the tilt of his head to follow the tilt of his brow.

"If I recall, I was about to ask an important question," His body seemed to slither and melt into the table without moving, the shadows played across the walls, he cast nothing there behind him, just void empty space.

"You…"

Interrupted again by Scarface (urp, sorry, Scarface Jock), "You wouldn't happen to be Tesse Slake would ya? The outlaw Tesse Slake?"

Tesse looks up from the gapping wound triumphantly, "Of course mister, who else would I be?"

Click and hammer pull.
Safety off.
Scarface on his feet.
Two guns out.

Legs straddle.
Head cocked.
One trained on Gummy.
One on Jess.

"N' I'm a'guessin' this here is ol' Gummy huh? Yeah, just stay where you are. Been on your trail since Spokane in '97. Me? I'm a bounty hunter of course. Here to take my reward."

Ken squints open one eye, casts it on Green, "A'bounie'hunner'c'n'you'belee'at?"

"*Unimaginable,*" Green moans, "*Simply* unimaginable. My question still remains gentlemen."

"Now you all just take this rope," Scarface Jock tosses a long hempen boa to Moe, "and go on tie these two up."

"But, Microfiche here?" A chorus of rough bum shouts.

"More a' you 'll be shot, if you don't get on," He waves the gun emphatically.

"Sorry about this sweetie," Packing whispers to Gummy as he wraps his wrists up.

Bums fumbling along knocking each other down falling over rope lines, spilling food across the floor, growing pale going red sweating out the wine they've been guzzling down, teetering, tottering, flushing, forgetting, Sawtooth started to wander off staring out the ceiling at the sky, recalled, moved back to the rope, Scarface wishing he could scratch the itch along his scar but with two guns trained and two bounties made there's no hope.

"You bums are right worthless, I have a mind to ask any way all you gathered here, who's in charge, who's the leader of this debouched train promenade?"

"I am," a voice we hadn't heard in a long while.

Who
    Was
        That
            Any
                Ways?

"I think you miscounted my friend," Forshmak grins seductively at Valentine, rubbing his nipples through the thin yellow fabric of his shirt.

"What the hell are you doing?"

"You still have one card."

"What? No."

Valentine looking down and there it is a 2 of hearts.

Forshmak Toot drops his last three cards over Valentine Green penultimate lofty piece. Car is silent refracted lights curtains drawn every eye looks including the two you can't see, he's been beat. Scarface is utterly confused, Tesse and Gummy tied up, Moe, Sawtooth tying, Microfiche bleeding out.

"It's me," Forshmak says sententiously, slowly rising from his chair, "I am the *President...the LEADER!*"

AND *bow.*

Indeed. Indeed.

Forshmak Toot is the King of all o' these folks.

Too bad there's open revolt.

The bums instantly turn foaming at the mouth like the zombie hoard, even poor Microfiche lurches to his feet out for the kill, they cover the space between themselves. Tesse and Gummy with less than super human strength (leave it to a drunken bum to tie a knot) break free and join the mob. Forshmak is set upon by the ravenous fist and feet, he's raised above their heads, hoisted, marched around.

"But, I'm your *leader*!"

Guess it wasn't in the cards, as the Rodman's say.

Scarface sets down to eat the rest of the food waiting for the action to die out before he reasserts himself.

"That's enough," Valentine lifts his strange Lovecrafted pistol and lets the bottom handle drop on the table on the pile of cards, "We ARE going to play this hand. Or else."

"Else what?" Scarface sneers.

VRRYYZZZAAAT! Blue microwave fire from the gun mouth. Scarface has no more scar no more skin no more muscle tendon veins no more bones no more clothes in fact cease to exist. Just the charred memory of an irascible man nobody will forget to miss. Not that kill'n him was in any way alright…

Braun and Ken sit up like some square at a board meeting neo-liberal feast.

"Now, that I've gotten your attention," cards shuffle by themselves, gun re-loaded and asserting, "Let's play this next hand."

"Whatever you say, boss, this graviton sinthe got my feet cemented to the floor, no place to go regardless, seeing we're on this here locomotive," Braun checks his cards, audible grunts, "Ya, better deal ol'Toot in still, I'm sure if he survives the onslaught he'd still like to play."

Khar-ghra-f'hgh'ra! Valentine (laughs? Cries?) ***H'ragy't'la!*** Whatever the hell of hells it was it surely was in delight.

"Certainly off-putting," Braun toasts the demon with another sip of gasoline.

"N'all'er'ight'altiny'reen," Ken, casually remarks yet to check the hand he's been dealt. Card watching hard the table surface laying facedown about an inch and unfathomable distance from the edge. Your guess on the strength of the hand is as good as Microfiche Cain's or Forshmak Toot's bloody lip.

But.

No.

Doubt.

    The cards

      like all the rest

     that came before

   Holy shit.

they're shit.

lost at the bottom of the world

I have an interesting proposition. A very intriguing rule. It seems you gentlemen know me. See, but, maybe I do or maybe I don't know you. As I have mentioned previously I am here on this very train because I am in search of two criminals, who are, for lack of a better word, escapees. Two vagabonds loose on this dimensional space left to spread open absurdity on this domain of rule and rigid accountable reality…what I mean to say is would you two *gentlemen* like the illusion of a choice on this next rule considering how easily I've won the preceding hands? The way I see it your decision is this. And it's very simple so please I beg of you do not over think it, do not consider and reconsider it, do not think on this lightly, but do not dwell on it. Your choice is this: You may either answer the question I asked as to your identities or I will propose a new state of reali—*Valentine Green, the monologue of*
CUT SHORT:

Ken puckers up ready to spit sane words. Braun leans out in front of the cataleptic drunk.

"Listen man," Braun teases confidentially, "We *know* why you're here okay?"

So you do, yes?

"Yeah."

Well then, why don't you enlighten *me?*

"You said you were here to catch two criminals right?"

I did…indeed. You seem to be catching up.

"…and I feel like we've come to a kind of understanding, maybe even something approaching a friendship while playing this here game."

Companionship? yes, go on…

"So I feel like I can confide to you something of great impact to your search."

and this would be?

"I don't wanna say it so loud."

Hmmm…

"Closer."

Hrmmm…

"Okay. Okay. I'll whisper it."

What is this that it would be so important that you had to whisper it?

"They might hear! (whisper-rasped)"

WHO?!

"Shhh."

Well?

"Okay. Here it goes."

YES!

"I'm ready."

OKAY!

"In a moment."

INDEED!

"Two names."

YOU DON'T SAY!?

"Tesse Slake and Gummy Joe Miles."

Tearsy Slakes and Gerny Joe Moles?

"Tesse Slake and Gummy Joe Miles."

Tesse Slake and Gummy Oh Moats?

"Right."

And?

"It's them!"

What? What about them?

"I'm'a'retty'sur'they'a'uns'a'outlaws'ur'look'in'fer!"

For Hells sake! Forget it! I've had enough of this pretense! This vile vaudeville act!

Braun wears a puppy dog face painted innocence stuffed under his beard hair drooping down. Ken looks at Green with weary eyes that drunken say ignorance is something that can't be traced wear it on your torn lapel and drag it through space. There's feigned withdraw on the walls of waking room, cut the tension, barometric pressure, hurricane swoon, Green shakes with anger the shit of the bounty hunter paper serve fuck the grimy game and the fucked up law that plays this way in circles cards are rectangles are finite angles asshole is a key the key to ending this debacle SEGUE TO: THE NEW RULE:

I tried to peel this from your bones nicely you insipid fools.

But you caused this climax and the end of every soul on this

godforsaken metal carcass. The new rule is this. The train

will spiral tighter and tighter down a newly hewn track

tighter and tighter in an ever decreasing spiral until it

implodes onto itself in a negatonic detonation that will send

its very existence into fiction with the caveat that there is no

way for you or your mendicant friends to prevent the

inevitable end. The bums will die yes. The conductors will

die of course. And you two simple men who seem to be so

familiar with me and torment my generosity will be

dropped into an interdimensional prison with no clear

sentence and no discernable timetable for release nothing

less than a terrible warped forever if I get my wish.

The train abruptly pulls up
tracks follow suit tearing
stone shod ground
locomotive leans on its side
picking up speed
bums hustled to the walls
like a gravitron ride
Toot thrown against the side
a shot of sinthe holding the Rodman boys in place
Green staring down no eyes through his nose
hate hate hate hate hate
the hellish stink of burning metal
rotting wood
open canned heat
spilt wine
diamond sky
moldy hamburger
vomited baked beans
the haunting laughter of the bounty
the closing grip of the machine

the last hope at the bottom of the world

flushed.

Rod man's Hand

one last hand
    Green's pistol smoking on the table
trigger in finger
    hammer in hand

Here we go again
    and this one's not even close
Green's teeth gaining
    sentient incisors howling along with the flip

of the card
    the doom
the remorse
    the program

Green sweeps away from his chest out to the Rodman hand,
Ken is face down in his own sleep Braun is watching
greedily at the one card left in the yellow fingers creaking
train reeking the speed is beginning to distort the air around
them the tracks burning up and melting in their wake
bowties lowties afterbirth roadtie double helix nighttime
nightmare freight fright inimical delight

Braun goes two palms up
    can't beat the hand and passes
Green tries to poker his smile
    but with those teeth no shot

this is how it goes down
or more like how it doesn't

"Hey," Forshmak Toot through the bloody nose, "I never got
to jettison my final card."

and in comes the two of heart.

"that's uh heh, that's a skipped turn."

Green laughs, it doesn't matter he only needs one more flip.

Ken sits up the skip goes to him, he's got 52 cards from the deck slid out from his sleeve.

"I guess I'll drop all of 'em," He says laughing soberly, "But one."

"What!" Green growls, "Impossible. Y~y~y~y~y~you cheat!"

but a cheat is one who's
a cheat is that one who
but he was never caught and how
the rules of Asshole go
if it's not on you it's on me

Oh No

that skips Green 35~36~ hmm something like 52 times
skips Braun too but he just laughs
case closed

and now Ken drops the last card

a plaid ace he's been dangling from his sleeve

fuck

"Mr. Green, my apologies sir, upon further investigation, you may have been conned."

the Asshole drinks the rest of the bottle of gravity sink, by presidential decree.

Green chuckles, you *Rodman* are fools. There's nothing left in the—

Well, now that the game is won
and the secret out

Ken turns to Braun shoulder shrugging, "I guess we should be going then, huh? Gotta get to the coast!"

                                   THE BOXCAR BOP

Green tugs the bottle hard, grunt, oil bubbling the whole
damn thing is full
to the very fucking unbelievable top but two sips worth gone

Braun goes heads up, Ken does the calculations in his head
just to keep our feet on the ground you know

sorry my man you've been had
the sinthe'll sink you to the lower realities or
down on the floor
where you'll be no more
as the train devours itself
funny thing
slight of hand
we've been drinking
nitro coffee this entre time
and Braun shakes the tankard from his sleeve
clang on the floor it rings hollow
no need for cream or sugar
always drink it black regardless
snap of long sharp teeth oppressive snapping
clenching sapping

down the gullet Green goes straight to the feet an untold-
tillion
pounds of gravity time distortion weight
into the ancient big bang of space-time
falling toward the center beginning
his body sinking faster than brain
his teeth rotting on sugar crimes
sweetness and power

Oh, fuck it, Green sneers forcing hands up
aiming twin guns, **Braun and Kenneth Rodman**

**for the crimes of inter-dimensional vagrancy fifty-two
counts
assuming false universal identities seventy-five counts
drinking black coffee without restraint uncountable counts**

skipping the inter~time~dilation turnpike toll seventy~seven
counts
hitching in a lower reality two counts this is a felony charge

for which you're both sentenced to unending ever~present
DEATH!

flash of hissing lasers boiling blue electric venom
bodies falling through time
warping the words playback rhyme

false uncountable fifty~two counts assuming black counts
assuming counts assuming uncountable seventy~seven
identities
turnpike counts of uncountable reality inter~dimensional
vagrancy
this inter~time~dilation counts skipping charge black of
coffee charge
uncountable inter~dimensional toil without toll

table blown into oblivion
Caaaaaaaaaaaan't piiiiiiiiiiiiiiiiiiiiicK up

PHRIIISHHHHHHHHHH!

Braun dives down his jacket seared at the elbows
Ken runs to the side of the car
it's getting hard to move
the train is winding down
ouroboros of itself
the center implosion imminent
n   o   t   i   m   e

COME ON YOU BUMS
Y   O   U   B   U   M   S
come on you bums

they claw and crawl

full black converse shoes. Office is perfect square,
no pictures on walls, minimal, hardwood floors desk
empty but for pen/notepad/sickly looking lamp

emitting cagey tired yellow light/typewriter
rundown old remington been lugged
the L stuck since 1979
chugged snapped pounded full
since birth ribbon almost
red white black blue

sound road
sorry for pome-for-pome bridge bit sorry
symbolically toe-to-toe step,
ditty little road browned stop, one—Rodman's
toe-to-toe feed this road for one old stop,
bridge lines, road little ends pounding stuck lyric-to-lyric,
mile step, road sing pounding for old they're literal for
literal trip's to lyric-to-lyric,
sing this this switch out this t   h   is   thi
s
t   h   i   s

gun blasts all around
ring off the ceiling torn
red heat fire through thighs and arms
and legs
beams smash to floor
blinds light up like ovens
seats overturn burn
Gummy gets one through the brain
prat falls dead
Tesse stoops down
leaning over her lost love
fights back an outlaw tear
rolls him over
picks his wallet & keys
takes Ken's hand

Moe says he's gonna stay
gotta see the other side
Sawtooth pleading c'mon man please
Braun grabs him by the underwear
hoists him up wedgey-anyway
tosses him out the door
Microfiche pulling his guts in

staple them shut or tie a beggar's knot be done
hobbling gets **SCKREEEEEEEEEEEE**
through the arm holy bitch god damn
full'a holes fer chrys'ake
with the inside torrent flashing out

Valentine losing shape
ivory bones fall from seer suit
misshapen thing oozing spikes
jagged teeth dipped in ice
raw running rotted blood

train streaking

On an oft quoted day in American world history when that
famous fissure in reality stabilized there were two f i g u
r e s   l   e   f   t

the last two to Jump

Braun on the left side door
Ken on the right

Green got them nailed in his sight
both pistols leaning

aim just a little off
singe the tweed from the back
Braun was hoisting Packing
out the hell into oblivion shape
Packing smack his lips
final memory the oil rich taste
of fried black swan skin
egg yolk boil

another chance breathe steady
his innards black hole descend
the well of his body
hold together hold to get them
out on the Kansas plain
junction city the car
I'll track them to that train

and there my trap

that isn't right he's
not there that was what sky
no trigger the train the car the game
shoot out into wheat fields glances
off the door frame
Tesse Moe and Microfiche fall out
into free~what could be~doom
from the sliding gate
bent toward other sides

As long as I plug you two it doesn't matter,
Valentine growls triumphant, just have to level the gun
the gun the gun the level the
time is collapsing and the trigger is lagging
behind level the gun
there's no time to drag the gun
before the trigger pull recoil

level the focus on tweed backs
steady the line the gun
lock the shoulder level
the gun level the shoulder
the gun the gun the gun

one stumble
one wrong step

P   O   W
e   n   d
b ut   th ough   ts   a r   e becoming
so   s   trench ed o   u   t

hey there yesterday
tempted to wait for the next act
curious if the characters recycle

round trip is revolving door caught on respawn

dialogue appears the same read along screen bottom

try to envision the clothes or the shoes
as they reappear each day
gently shaded
slid along the gradients
placed under same drawn faces
pre-loaded conversations
vagueness of expression

I am through with memetic creation

the pie of the world is a single universal color and only a
few leftover Kbs remain

sky is a background barely noticed in clear days

I am an absentee programmer alone at the keys

tempted to wait for the next act
tempted to wait for the next act

tempted to
tempted to

witness the internal error

external relation
internal value alue   alue

error
tempted to
tempted to wait

witness the
recycle re cycle cycle ycle ycle
ycle

act

level the

gun level the

'Of all the gol' dang universes in all the tripping falling
hypertime realities of this spinning bluey-green sphere, he
had to collapse in this one,' Ken thought

the gun

thought that before
entering old body old mind old memory
circling back level

they move along the cabin wall
prying the bums free
turning upright chairs

As long as I plug you two it doesn't matter,
Green growls triumphant, just have to level the gun
time is collapsing and the trigger is lagging behind
there's no time to drag the gun
before the trigger pull level

flushing spiral force of the train pushed the Rodmans to the
door
strength of the dreamwood worms pulled Valentine Green
down
down d o w   n do   w n
d   o   w   n

Ken flips his chromatic coin on the leash snap free
the light flashes blinds the no eye
metal tick and tink off fleshy demon face
one dented tooth no toothpaste

the last tattered garments of life in the
personage of Sawtooth Puddin' leap into no space
now the car is clear only the feel of
suffering stench feet sunk to floor
traveling slowly backward in time

what's se ei n   g st   rai   gh   t

they're both hands on metal doors
heads turned back

smirking

not at Valentine Green

"Heard somebody ordered two criminals, two worthless,
rambling, pariahs? Well here they are for ya!"

my life for

two perfect shots

imposing and dripping metal

DEATH DEATH LEVEL DEATH GUN

two perfect misses spiral into space

empty

before they go Toot wanders through the cabin
wtf come on doffs his cap scratches his head
wounded eyes of the teary animal glances up
what if I left something behind dives into the
drowning snake mouth toot check'n gone
we're gonna have to leave you
Ken scratches his chin motions to the warped stars
Braun waves his hand into chaos go ahead yo   u f ir s
t...

The Rodmans nod one final good bye to the lost Toot weary
left Braun i   s hands fla i ling goooooo o o   o ne be at
j   u   m   p out   into
th   e   aby   ss
nothing no   ting   non   thing
the tra   in tig   hter   tigh   ter
Ken o   ne   la   s   t   lo   n   g
l   oo k   m ight ha ve double to o   k a   t hi   s
l uc ky   co   in   laid across   Val   en tine   's
fa   c   e
w   a

          ve   s   a   s ad   vau   dev
ille   good   by   e
jettisons   in   t   o n   ev   erne   ss

time   time time time time time time time time time time
time time

 time time time time time time time time ti

me time time time time time

 time time time time time time time time time tim
e time time time time halting motions for the check like
they're moving
out and they are, they've occupied one single table, time
time time time
 time time time time time time time time time t
ime time time time time time time time time time time
 time time time timetimetimetime time tim
e time tim
e time time time time time time time time t
ime time time time time waspinkraspberriesovertheunder
clouds
as they sayandthesailingbehemoth time time tim
e time time   time   time   time   time
tim
e   time   time   time   time timetimetimetime   tim
e time time time time time time time time time
time time time ti
me time time time time
time time time time time time   looser
looser   looser   loo   lo
looservvvvvv looser looser looser looser looser looser looser
looser looser looser looser looser looser looser looser There's
stars shooting forth and breaks and screeching awful smells
rubber burning rubber smells looser looser loos and those
cars spin out on prairie route I-70 going through red sky
Kansas City looser looser looser looser looser looser looser
looser looser looser looser looser looser looser looser looser
looser looser looser looser looser looser looser looser looser

looser looser looser looser looser looser looser looser looser
looser looser looser looser looser loo

ser

loo

looser looser level looser looser looser looser

looser
looser looser lo

oser loos

er
looser loo

ser coiling line coiling rail lines train coil train line melt
melt lines train coiling coiling train coiling coil train lines
train coil coil coil coiling lines coiling coiling railing coil
train lines rail lines coiling coiling train coiling rail line coil
train "Doesn't sound anything like me," He shrugs, Ken is
off and listening in the past knowing the game is on the
loose and down railing melt melting tighter heavier sinking
falling through time lines dimension lines fault lines arrow
lines sinking into soup abyss abstract fifth space hulking
coiling rail lines into self ouroboros alternate parallel heated
melting train hulking parallel heavier lines through coiling
lines coil into coil coiling fifth parallel coil dimension coil
coiling coiling melt lines Clear your mind, listen and you'll
hear an almost inaudible sundering sizzle of air, of friction
on swishing Whitman-like leaves of grass, sniff for a slight
burning smell in the air, minute sparks of reality gasp and
implode, die out, dried, like the bubbling on Yellowstone
ledges like the sulfur smell of the damned abstract lines self
train lines lines coiling through rail rail fault rail coil lines
lines lines train coiling into coiling train train coiling
sinking coil train melt coil coil coil abstract coil train
abstract line soup lines line into r ail sinking soup coiling
rail melt lines coiling m elt t   ra in c   o i l in g train
train self   ra   I   l p   ara   ll   el loos   er re
ali   t   y

lo   o   o   o s   e   r   t
i   g   ght   er
t h   e   tr   a   in   i m
plooo   o   ding   on   i t   '   s
own   weight   v a ni   sh   es   tr
a   in   i m   plooo   o   ding
time on   i t   '   s   own a   in
i m   plooo   o   looser   ding   on   time   i t
'   s   own   weight   v a ni   sh   es
tr   a   All aboard--the ste   amer RO
DMAN   U.S.S
making   all   LO-CAL   Sto   pS He
re's th   e   honest tru   th of the m   atter spilt ou
t spelled ou   t cl   ad o   ut—
We   are   the   old   things that   must
die and   go   away   to be   reborn
 in   i m   plooo   o   time   ding
time
a   in   i m   plooo   o   ding
on   i t   '   s   own   weight   v a ni
sh   es   tr   a   U.S.S making LO-CAL all
RODMAN aboard--the steam   er st   eamer
STOP   in   i m   plooo   o   ding
P   OP   POP   P   O   P   O
P   O   P
P O   P

P   O   P

P   O   P

P O

P

P O

P

POP

P

O

P

*Stop—implode

Hyperloop Hustle
one/I ought'a pick you two up on vagrancy;

NO
Loitering
Soliciting
Trespassing
or
Panhandling

An Hysterical Drama
Breaking camp outside Wells, NV
morning light dulls night fire still a'smoke
wells is burning my lord wells is burning bright
the bums cleared out around 5 am
left a bottle of wine half full without a note
selfless present leaning on the old log bench
dragging sticks tethered to their clothes
they must have left in the dawn shimmering
fast and woody bent toward the west

east an hour earlier sunken into salt flat
authorities discovered the missing railroad tracks
but the car they'd never find
the salt had filled in the footprints of last survivors
left not a shred of evidence
not one rusted gutted bolt

in between the laser sheered lay lines
a hole of holy clay 100 acres in diameter
at its center sloshing through the exposed belly
the FBI discovered a single evergreen tree
encased in salt it was dated to about 400 years
it hadn't appeared on any ring map

the case was left cold indeterminately
linked to a confused paper trail of the past
on the internet it sparked a 24 hour controversy
until like snopes flashed mush it was laid to rest
as uncorroborated by AP there was no good reason
as anyone could readily admit to pursue further

the inane idea of time travelers
the salt made its slow trek back into white obscurity
and invariably the holy hole sealed itself and memory up

Book Jacket
"The vagrant has been threatened with every species of
punishment known to the law, and he has at different times
been stocked, scourged, branded, imprisoned, and hanged,
but he still survives with his old tricks as merrily as ever...no
sooner has he become practically acquainted with any new
law or regulation intended to repress him than he rises
superior to it..."
~ C.J Ribton Turner, *A History of Vagrants and Vagrancy
and Beggars and Begging*

"They [skid row men] are frequently interesting and
charming people, but they are generally incapable of
forming durable, satisfying, or, in a psycho-therapeutic
sense, useful personal relations."
~ J.P Brantner quoted in, Leonard Blumberg, Thomas E.
Shipley, and Irving W. Shandlet, *Skid Row and Its
Alternatives: Research and Recommendations from
Philadelphia*

"Skid Row…is a slang term for a dilapidated stretch or
section of a town, origin from 'skid road', used by loggers
and lumber people for a greased log road which newly cut
logs are dragged, in use as early as 1880. Madison St. in
Chicago and the Bowery in New York City are also referred
to as skid rows."
~Excerpt from the *Philadelphia Inquirer*, June 22, 1966

"It's like that damn sword, that damn sword of Demascus
[sic], hangin' over our heads for all this time…we're being
pushed out, no place to go; just waiting for the sword to
fall."
~Charlie, Skid Row resident about the demolition of his cage
motel

lifted from Wikipedia for reference
Wells is a small city in Elko County, in northeast Nevada in the western United States. The population was 1,292 at the 2010 census. Wells is located at the junction of Interstate 80 and U.S. Route 93, approximately 50 miles (80 km) east of Elko and is part of the Elko micropolitan area.

The site of Wells began as a place called Humboldt Wells along the trail to California. It was subsequently founded as a railroad town along the original Transcontinental Railroad, and was once a stopover for passenger trains. The Humboldt River has its source in springs and a swampy area just west of the city that today is called Humboldt Wells. In the late 19th century, Humboldt Wells was burning down, and in a frantic plea for help, a telegraph was sent that said, "Wells is burning".

Do not
lie or otherwise
be in a
horizontal
position on
a park bench
do not
sleep or remain

in any bushes,
shrubs or foliage

two/'but sir, that's an antiquated charge'

*so that you pulled your knees up to your chin
blind to dirt and dust and scruff and tar*

spit back up
Down from the mountain relieved of all their earthly
possession the Rodman pair stalked on soleless shoe and
tattered heal down down the barren hills and into
downtown Wells, their clothes torn and grayed their faces
caked with baptismal dust of the high desert scar. In regular
fashion and without restraint they accosted the first diner
they saw.

outside red white blue lights howled

—couple a bums in here askin' about coffee, the proprietor
nasaled into phone

loaded up and peeling out at 105 three squad cars cut in
heating the pavement rolling from three long western blocks
away
hands on guns itchy doors give that metal lip creak
reports coming a few months ago and 40 years hence
had placed these men in junction maybe
on the run maybe armed maybe dangerous maybe
they fit the description maybe lowdown baby

they were begging was all that needed to be known

diner door potato chip thin
swings out against the wind
silent and marked inside
by palm print grease

along the booths the boots beat
on the ground combat ready

to the table in the back

where the boys been set up

leaning out over the faces
stomach leaning from belt
toothpick leaning from lips
eyes leering behind tinted lens
fingers hooked into belt
thumb on pistol release

Braun and Kenneth
weary and just been served
two steaming hot cups
warming their blackened fingers
glance up into the beige and starry void

bums, greeted sheriff Jones
officer, greeted the bums
he tap his badge light
sheriff, greeted the bums

offer of coffee, again the bums, just a sip
we've had a long night I think you'll agree?

no thanks, Jones waved them off
insinuating laughter directed to his backup,
hey, ah what's that next to you on the seat?

what this? a tilted bottle ruby *chianti* uncorked
a gift from friends long gone

open bottle of dago red looks like to me, Jones said
holding up his own gift, two shiny pair of cuffs,

but, sir that's an antiquated charge, they appealed

not here in my city, in my state, he got tough, and certainly
not in this here year of the lord 19 god damn n' 38

that was the kicker they conversed in tongue, jabbering
along, in modern verse, the train the implosion the inter-
generational kick, jumping out we'd missed the boat

sir, I apologize, said Braun, we're a couple'a dead ones

sir, *We* apologize, said Ken, you see this is all a big
misunderstanding a big mistake…

Yeh? Jones grunted checking his partner Deputy Myers by
slant eye

Myers giggled fiddling with an unlit cigarette,
rough pig thoughts like,
seems these boys r'gonna put up a fight

…You, see… Braun—ze set-up

…We've accidently traveled backward through time, Ken—
ze knocked'em down

so that you took to running knifed edges across grain
drawing up curled veins

That phone call
operator: Hello. This is the Elko County Sheriff's Department
please state your emergency.
caller: there's a couple of uh bums barged in here.
dangerous. they looks dangerous.
operator: can I have your name and location sir?
caller: of course! I am the owner and pro—
operator: your *name* and loc—
caller: I am the owner and—
operator: your name and location s—
caller: I am the *owner* and propri—
operator: go ahead sir
caller: owner and proprietor of the Famous Jules' Diner in
Wells my name is Howland Thompkins and my fine and
family owned establishment is located right off the corner
of—
operator: I know where the diner is sir, what's your
emergency?
caller: Like I said there's two bums here, drunk if you ask
me, they are endangering my-my business! and my-my-my
customers! it's the morning rush! this is a matter of life and
death!

operator: can you describe the two men?
caller: describe them!? My word this is madness!
operator: …
caller: I dunno uh medium height? long hair? wearing
tweed suits…uh…oh sitting down in the back tried to put
them out of the way so's it's hard to see… they're uh they're
covered in dirt or clay or something there's clouds of it
clomps of it everywhere in their hair on their clothes
covering their faces…oh and they have beards bunch'a bum
rowdies most like out to rob me I tell you, look at em! now
you better—
operator: officers have already been dispatched to your
location. hang tight sir.
caller: oh you're god damn right I will and this better not
cost me—
operator: good bye sir and have a wonderful rest of your
day.
caller: well I—!

*so that each needled point penetrated the skin
and left glitters of light in their path*

jailhouse
but but but but to be honest sir but ya gotta but
pay your bill at the register shift that light as air door
and count about 58 seconds of wait outside by your
automobile
they were forcibly removed from the coffee mugs posthaste
taken out to the squad car down the crumbling cement steps
and driven directly to the center of town where the station
lie
they were booked on several charges: disturbing the peace,
vagrancy, public indecency, public intoxication,
possession of illegal or illicit substances,
and most importantly, and foremost of all, resisting arrest

Aw c'mon, they moaned from the wrong side of the pen
barred prison state
lock'em up dry'em out holding tank pay to play real estate
grafting gangbang

man, this is gonna be a weird anti-climactic 70 year sit and wait

Case No#: 0002361KNBR

"On October 15, 1938 subjects were apprehended outside Jule's Diner in Wells, NV. They possessed no valid identification and local authorities first believing them to be migrant workers locked them up on charges of public drunkenness and vagrancy. It wasn't until the discovery of the strange **[REDACTED]** crash in the Utah Salt Flats that these men came to our attention as possibly **[REDACTED]** involved. On their persons they possessed nothing extraordinary (listed below) but their story was curious enough to warrant a more intense study. There is at this time no hard evidence connecting them to **case no# 0002357TRN**.

"Outright they professed to be from the year **[REDACTED]**. The same year printed on the serial number discovered amongst the wreckage. In opposition to repeated urging of a relaxed sentence if they were to cooperate they refused to aid the investigation any further and subsequent interrogation failed to produce any new leads. Their last statement given separately was the exact same sentence that… 'the mystery would be solved when the [REDACTED] crashed [REDACTED] years from now in [REDACTED].' The 'brothers' have been since moved to a Federal Penitentiary in Carson City, Nevada where they await charges of obstruction to a Federal Investigation.

"In the case of the [REDACTED], all remnants have been taken to an off-site FBI facility for storage. No further eyewitnesses or evidence as to the origin of both the brothers and the [REDACTED] has since come to light.

"As of November 17, 1950 **ND#0002361KNBR** has been designated a cold case to be reopened pending approval no earlier than the date of October 15, 20[REDACTED]."

*so that at night it appeared as it did before
but for the metallic taste*

intergalactic hitch
hollow skeleton hobo
poets hang on branches
in the sun, weightless
like bird's wings
flapping old toothless

jaws, readin' with
archaic sounds,
swinging torn shoes,
biting tin collars,

up on the wire
handkerchief to break
impending fall, over
all beady heads
singing songs,

tweed jackets like
lightning spark up
a breeze, a fantasy
shower, there's not much
left in this dimension gate,
they gotta be going,
no one listening, no one
believing,

there, out there,
beyond that golden orb
is another gal~
axy far gone

ears and eyes
to turn on

flowers to give
gardens to sow.

baggage
Items recovered from the persons, Kenneth and Braun
Rodman:

- two fountain pens (no ink)
- half a moleskin notebook (unlined; empty)
- one small glass vial containing (in varying
    amounts): mud from the shore of the Mississippi
    river, needles from the *Pseudotsuga menziesii*,
    commonly known as **Douglas fir**, several pebbles
    from the Rocky Mountains, prairie grass from

Kansas and Iowa, clay from the Utah Salt flats, sand
from the painted desert in Arizona, dried saguaro
cacti chips, dried crumbs of peyote and marijuana
plant
~   car key of unknown model and make

*so that even though your outside mildewed with collapse
the inside shone brightly in the sun*

panopticon

"I was just having my morning coffee you know, like I
always do, one dollop of cream, no sugar, before my shift
you know, and that's when they come in all covered in hard
clay, smelling like god knows what, looking for a booth.
Well, I pointed them off to Beth, see as I wasn't starting
yet…"

"They ordered two cups of coffee and two glasses of
water…"

"…Drunk, they was dead drunk I tell ya, like every bum
coming through town, botherin' people pressing
hardworking Americans that can barely afford to live for
change. We got the call so we hurried over there to take'em
in to lockdown like we usually do so they can clean up and
get moving on, we ain't got any room to let the likes of them
sleep around here…"

"Bums. They was lousy bums."

…and the floorboards were golden

Poem left at Rodman Camp

"Down on luck. Spare a buck?"

"Have you ever felt invisible before?"
"Can you spare a quarter?"

"Anything helps."

"Need food. Please help."

"Can you spare a dime?"

"Anything helps."

"You ever had invisible food?"
      "Anything you ever had."

"A buck helps."

      "Anything like a buck?"
"Invisible before a dime."

"Need food luck change. Please spare."

"Have you ever felt invisible before?"
      "Please anything helps."

"I'm sorry I don't have any cash on me."

drunk on diamonds
next night somewhen under the stars, no matter what year,

the milky way wrapped about their heads like a halo shroud,

the sky a barrel of diamond turned upside down, the fire

kicking long shadows against the trees making a crown of

the mountain of the earth around, they sat and marked a

toast to the two phantoms they'd left, they toured the bottles

around like a venn diagram counter-clockwise and its twin

the opposite way. By the time the sun shone its face and

bleary faded the night they were dead drunk slumped over

in the dawn, Tesse was the only heart holding on when with

eyes closed to the indifferent though never inimical earth

she couldn't help but sing:

> *while I was drinking wine, honey,*
> *I thought that I had died, honey*
>
> *while I was drinking wine*
> *you see*
> *while I was drinking wine*
>
> *I thought that I had died, honey*
> *at the last drop of wine, honey,*
>
> *at the last drop of wine*
>
> *at the last drop of wine*

One Long Road Poem

transcontinental hitchhike

nothing left of the cops but melted faces,
what the hell
fuckers would have been let off easy,
administrative leave or something

but jesus, nobody deserved that-and that
had spoken
couldn't understand it-**What is epilogue has
no beginning**
dunno just thought of it and it sounds
cool, also-
**there was only a sinking sense of murmuring
desolation,
west, which is the only destination left,
west which is the only direction**

luckily by dawn a town crept up-Junction
City-
not sure how many miles I walked but it's
been hours
aside from whistles and stares it's
alright, speeding cars
these fucking family men yelling she had no
ass and faggot hair
hard-ons jerking off

shouldn't have bothered with hotels,
there's no rooms,

stacey's was the clue-**there was a gentle
orgasm glow about the place
something lingering there and slowly
fading, innocent-**

at the counter I asked 'Mary Beth James'
about the two bums,

described their state of grace, she flashed
like a cash register in her eyes,

'well-hun-(glancing up I was waiting for
it) oh son-er-
did you want a table, oh?' she had to
qualify it, whatever,

got an egg sandwich on muffin no cheese no
hash browns some fries to go
stuffed it in my pack, only have 250 bucks,
now 247.50 to spend

she could barely hide the 'thank god' look
on her face that I wasn't staying
made a check over the counter the booths
fucking nerve to say
'probably should get moving out of town if
you know what's good fer ya,'
under her breath

west on 70 then toward the great salt
lake-**hope my atlas hold up**

shit, outside town 2 miles (?) sitting
behind an old road sign about to unwrap
lunch
leaning on the old fender of a buick 197-
maybe 2
bitch is sinking into an endless rot but I
think if I can get it back to town-
the windows, doors unlocked, no key in the
ignition, gotta be abandoned
pushing it down 40 is gonna suck-

first whistles about five minutes in,
bearing down like 18 wheel truck,
not the first car won't be the last-
'hey baby, how's about-' **I don't wear a
mask, this is me**

horn honks guys think they can flirt from
the driver's side from behind
undressing cupping my ass, my legs their
fucking eyes
dyke faggot bitch ass pussy abomination
bible quote
fairy punk law of the land from the front

**from the whining seat of a rolling car
any body is tits ass cock pussy dickgirl
honey cuntboy baby**

took a few hours to make it to town
the junkyard covered in grease
repairs on the down low not cheap
how bout by the refrigerator in the back,
honey
real quick half off, suck a dick faggot

-no, but thanks

you look alone the eyes and goatee say
but here's a roll of 20s what with cash no
paper trail
go down to 36 bucks- and it was 36 hours to
fix
coincidence-sitting in the junkyard
curling in the junk yeard under a blanket
roll
the odd orange lights barely there night
ain't even got a book to get a fix

in the morning the car was alive roaring
sputtering roaring but as long as it
doesn't overheat
**what more from these failing machines could
you ask?**

drove the rest of Kansas on cruise control
straight
no turns touched no pedals snapping flat
photos taking notes

finally ate the soaked cold moist egg
sandwich
speeding on one leg toward Colorado welcome
signs
gone gone Kansas golden high plains-
**fuck you hill of Golgotha and your 3
crosses every 10 miles-**

finally the wheat grows short I can see the
rock of earth pressing cutting jutting the
terrain
breaking free jagged misshapen-it's natural
beautiful
enduring-what I'd hoped
still each gas station casts sinister light
each squad car easing in behind pulling off
each leer of gaze from the next car's
backseat

-for a moment I'm alone 11,300 feet!
Berthoud Pass! snow cap peaks!
over the quiet snowy towns parallel the
railroad tracks
I know they must have hopped a train

can't remember any town names-note to look
back at the atlas
tried repeating them-ending with spring
rocky spring-
down the hills before you notice and the
day is out
the desert now the salt of the lake

at night I stopped to sleep near grandeur
peak-no artificial light

there are more stars than sky, and in the
morning the desert peaks rise up
as ghosts out of the dark!-I felt them but
couldn't believe they were there!
they glow a million rainbow colors in the
sunrise

Cruised through Salt Lake without stopping
birds playing frozen on the shore
I never considered the white nothingness of
the flats
only the ocean and the mountains and vague
understanding desert heat in my heart
but now glaring up like a mirror to the sun
I was here the ends of the earth
there was something like a black hole
strange blinking out
something with the same sense as the diner
2k miles back in the distance toward the
hills

I pull over into the deep cracking salt the
clay underneath sodden with ancient rain,
clay fucking sucked my shoes up, had to
leave them, fucking loved those shoes
dammit
my stomach dropped I was approaching the
railroad line
or what was left? Sudden gulf of a perfect
crop circle shape
the salt of the earth the lines the rail
the stone fasteners sleepers underlying
subgrade
not torn from the earth just vanished like
cut by laser to the pool of clay like a
plugged whirlpool

I felt sick, light-headed, dizzy, crossing
but I had to make it to the center

as a walked the clay sealed my foot prints
up behind me, weird fucking shit
a tiny wet napkin sinking in the mud I
picked it up between thumb and forefinger
on it was written in badly scrawled hand-

38.797153, -119.980810 ca.1938
NEED A LIFT ~KBR

-whatever the fuck that meant, coordinates
maybe looked like-no service-
can't even check-only thing about America-
you can literally drive straight across it
and never run into wifi
-under the napkin was a pine needle so I
pulled at it, sounds ridiculous but it
wouldn't come up
down on my knees in hardening clay until a
branch
the top of a tree more branches a fucking
trunk I pulled the thing until it came out
at about 3 feet
-In the car now, caked in hard mud up to my
knees, can't get it off my hands or face
When I stop for gas I'll clean it but not
now, when I get to Nevada I guess

on E I pulled off to a roadside station had
an old dial up tanker,
in every direction, all alone, by myself-
horizon nearly sunk below sea
-never feel good about this
inside at the counter dreadlocked white
hair and a long beard
I waited for his eyes to search my body but
they locked on mine
-'I'll fill'er up while you clean up,' he
said and handed me the keys without a
glance

**-what this fucker have
a camera in the
bathroom?** -washed anyway
the clay dropping slowly from my body
peeling almost, revealing me that had
drowned in mud-
**that had pulled an evergreen from the
abyss**-revealing me
that beyond the clay or soaked in it-me who
was not lost

He wasn't at the counter when I opened the
door
when I walked back to the car, he wasn't at
the pump either
inside there was a note on the dash in a
thin painstaking scrawl

-o n   t h e   h o u s e   ~d a v i d

In my rearview as I drove away David came
running behind me
struggling to hold something in his arms, I
eased the car to stop
'I'm an artist,' he said teary eyed,
panting,
'the gas pump it's only for rent,
I ran to the orchard in the back,
my wife, she used to have a garden, it's
still there but,
h e r e ,' he said into the window,
he handed me an arms full of apples, 'take
these,'
dark red, almost violet, blotched with
white-'For the road,' he said

as I pulled away west dust kicking up
he yelled jumping out of the past **'Road
Magic! Road Magic!'**

and I swear for a second I almost thought I
heard him shout my name
fucking crazy saint, he was like a maniac
'try the strawberries,'
he yelled, 'promise to try the
strawberries!'

the strawberries?-

but it was too late
I w a s for the road

I was picking up speed
chasing the wifi down.

Bookends; tattered ends; elbow pads

So it is that sentences end and old men are returned to them the possessions of young men taken uncountable years ago. So it is that old men seek to understand those young men and why they had discarded their possessions all those uncountable years ago. The last gift of the prison state a free of charge drive several miles on a rickety white bus, jettisoned on the side of the road two old bums south of opal colored lakes, sail boats, resort shakes. Driver points to stop sign red hexagon, so long, this is as far as owed to you, now scramble off you go. There's no bench, no awning escape from the incoming snow. The curb will have to do. The coordinates marked exactly a small road shoulder just east of lumpy waterhouse peak that at the same moment was being keyed into a smart phone several lovely miles away.

After the booking and the 70 years solitary confinement for wrongful arrest obstruction of justice audacity to protest, thoughts on social media mendicants pour out into the lock-up void, the fluorescent welfare seats, the forgotten shameful space. She's got one set of ambiguous clothes marked like the three thousand miles on the map and what are you questions unnecessary from the lost indigo violent horde, so much so she doesn't know how to answer when the car pulls around. To hate sex is to talk about it constantly, last fateful final words. Remember the little ones brains scooped out with prescription pills and shame. Happiness is not a state that can exist.

Check over your shoulder elbow shrug and inside wires
twist. This car is one way gone for the coast and after it's
flashed and disappeared what was once a rearview view is no
more. It was the anchorman pulled the trigger positioned pistol
out at the backdoor that's how they cheesed them hundred
two hundred four hundred years or more. Like clockwork,
cold, calculate.

> out by desert time climbing
> and the Mojave salt flat snow,
> continue west gaining elevation,
> Sierra Nevada peaks, cloud mountains
> peering down, high high evergreens
> sprouting pine cones, rushing glacial streams,
> two bums by side of road,
> old old bums, gray beards,
> chins hunched over knees.

That's where ya picked them up, that's where she slid open
the door—"the coast?" they shook their heads slow—"well
then, hop to it and get it! Ya don't look like you two ever caught
a freight in your life!" She said, letting the car roll so they'd
chase an aged chipmunk skittering in the shotgun seat, "You'll
freeze to death out here, ya damn vagrants!"

> "We're old skeleton men,
> thoughts that have become fiction,
> haven't seen the souls on earth in many days,"
> said the taller of the two. He leaned on the window
> frame
> followed along over each step with his feet.

> "Yah, lugs gonna get in or what," She laughed, "I got a
> date with the coastline!"

> at last prompted to action
> the old men groaned, slid in

car still a'rollin' they gently eased the door closed
sat for a while in silence, snow melt
shaking the cold, ruminating on loose eyeballs of
thought
10,000 feet up and swimming backward in their ancient
heads,

"Lucky you picked us up," the other,
He fidgeted in his seat. Fixed his back,
unbuckled his seatbelt, re-clamped the thing a dozen
times.
"we been stuck out in this s-s-s-s-storm
for p-p-probably, I'd say…f-f-f-forty, fifty year.
They don't make snow like they used to 1937 er 1938."

"Well I can take you as far as you want to go. Me, if you
must know, I'm gonna see the blue! Been waiting my whole
life to see her!" She said and they nodded in tired assent
sinking into the upholstery becoming part and one with the
sunken backseat.

the only movement she felt behind her head
the creak and sway of a vial round the neck
of the grey most slumped, both pair of shoulder
seemed to move imperceptible but solidly
along with the grayed out contents of the small
fragile crystal weighing on their decayed existence,

"What's that?" She said without turning to look back. They
groped and gapped with toothless gums, struggling to pierce
the meaningfulness of her questioning. "Around your neck?
What is it?" She asked.

"This?" They both at once passed forgetful
fingers lovingly, anemically, wretchedly
without glancing down as if once it was
realized, once it way made to be
it would cease forever to exist, "This?"
they croaked as children of someplace

long ago lost into the great mist
and conveyor belt of time, "This?"

"Yes, around your neck," She replied with genuine
affection, "What is it?"

"This," they mumbled together, gums gnashing
so that it was difficult to discern which if either
were speaking, the sound seemed to come from
the very contents of the vial of dust and gone things,
"This," they muttered slurred and groaned,
"This is the only evidence on earth that we ever lived."

From there they climbed down those mysterious hills descending in silence, leaning into the sharp curves, bent on the white line, canyons opening up, closing, lines of unbreakable unending trees, vast acres of quiet unknown forest, darkness and light and something everlasting, and all this time the car remote and small a speck on the face of the great wilderness at the edge of America on the last great range and after what becomes of us but the sea. The weight of the silence in the car was great and shadowed and bent the axles and worked the wheels and pushed against the windows and took in the crisp pure wind and reached out and gorged on the sun. She lit a cigarette, homemade, bit of green sprinkled in. She inhaled deep on the silence, on the plant, on life, of life, became of the living and dying and the clouds returned her thoughts, mountainous and raised above the world, to the weariness and wonder of the spinning orb, the gentle lean and gush of entropy and the beautiful rags wrapped upon it, everlasting and indomitable, rushing in the night like the haunting glow of the moon, the sadness of the stars ever deepening, the widening gulf of loneliness set forth upon humanity and visible as rocks rushing up to meet them to cup them to humble them in their silent grasp, she exhaled and the car expanded, creaking against its own weight and outside the sky opened up, closed, lines of unbreakable unending peaks, vast acres of quiet impenetrable wood, night and day and something unknowable, and all this time the car invisible but irrevocable on the surface of the great mountains at the end of America the last great forgotten rise and from it down down down until the vale lifts against the fog leaving only the sea the sea the blue heaven of the sea endless, infinite, and everlasting the sea, the sea, the blue heaven of the sea down hell bent from the mountains and stretching west and curling over the globe down down down from the green of deathless trees scored by fire witness to the short and sorrowful and glorious lives that crawl upon them love upon them lust upon them die upon them alone and forgotten and remembered and loved, down down from the mount to the sea to pursue the sea to the blue wonder of the heaven of the sea the sea down down to the sea the sea the blue blue heaven of the sea.

"You don't remember me?" She asked, shattering the hours of silence with her voice like a crash like an avalanche and the snow of the peaks held their breath and clung to the craggy rocks that are their birth that titter on the edge of existence, silent mourners of time, hitting the gas hard and picking up speed before they could spit tooth or word and sheheyou thought back, and without waiting for a reply answered with her own loving laugh, the dummies riding quiet in the lobotomized backseat, showered her with blank eyed stares and slack jaw wheat by the rearview way, "well, fuck. These old men out of time and space never do."

> into fields of bright beating red
> strawberries picked bloated gravid on the vine
> moved to small hunkered bowing wood shacks
> from vine to hand to hand to mouth
> the car eased and screeched to its only stop

"Hungry?" She said launching herself from the car, scrambled legs of a thousand miles drive, and back and bumbling over and brimming glowing hue of golden red on face and smeared with the blood red sweetness of the fleshy growth below the green, "Want some?" she leaned the paper carton into the back, the berry seeming to burst to be encased by some divine phantasmal thing, to be too bright for seeing, to be unreal in their utter realness, the old men took one each, the first of the berries was placed upon the mouth of the vial and slowly, juices snaking up the callused old square finger, down into the ampoule and becoming one with the varied contents as the seeded ovaries and mushed red coiled and soaked the contents, she noticed pine needles, salt flat clay, river mud of the Mississippi, god inducing plants, tiny turned stones of the rocky peaks, pink and yellow and white hues of the painted deserts the whole of a small speck of America turned up and pressed safely into that vial and as the last of the juices coalesced the vanishing colors again, the deadening to gray again, and the sucking of their fingers as they shared the other berry, as their faces, pock marked, bearded and smeared with brown mud and red life, stared back at her with blue eyes like ocean waves, "Pretty good, huh? I always wanted to taste a California strawberry right from the fields," she chewed another as she spoke, not even attempting to remove the plant like fur along the top, "Pretty good, huh? I'm ruined for strawberries for life, I think." And the car lighted along its way brake and all gunning the last miles across the gravel to the goal the sweet ever-present scent of sugar and red and berry replacing the pout of the gas and the burning of the head gasket and the engine choked and howled and kept going going going.

> and eventually there it was, the green aegis,
> the white hot gash of 1 and the coast,
> it was like reading this line, dropping them off
> at the long blue pacific cliffs ahead, for
> inevitably there, the end of the continent lay,
> and they had made it, and the fall had told them so
> the last cliff before the melancholy end
>
> there was no west left to go—
>
> sky sunk to pitch blue water
> depthless fathomless water
> obscure in the memory
> gleaming in the future
> incomprehensible in the now
> forever in its fathomless depth
> the sea the sea the endless sea
>
> on the unpaved shoulder
> the car stopped its second time
> three bodies slid out
> three faces toward the wild blue
>
> at the perilous edge
> they placed their feet
> crashing waves below 200 feet

the wind blew back the surf
making streaks of rainbow
in their darling eyes

"I always thought, when I got to the coast that I'd be able to dive right in like in a movie," She mused with ironic mirth, "hrm, here it is, it's better this way, I think" she said, rocking on her toes, testing fate, "the big land to the south. Here it is!" She shouted holding out her hands taking in the void of nothing no more land.

She stepped back, took out her phone, a selfie to remember me by, the pacific and me. The old men were huddled together, not speaking but conversing somehow, she stepped back to frame of photo of the sad hunched figures and the perfect cloudless sky the perfect immaculate ocean. At the click she could almost hear them counting down, for a moment she feared they'd planned to fall but there was something else, they waved their arms in a broken throwing motion and it was there she saw it sail, the vial tumbling down two hundred feet into the flashing unassailable waves of Big Sur, glittering in the sun it tumbled, slowly the dust the debris of a thousand lifetimes of a thousand Americas poured out trickled out clotted and broke and rushed and turned and fell and fell and vanished in the white slush of the breaking murderous beautiful waves and was gone and unchanged and forever and forever and forgotten.

"Do you want to go down to the beach she asked?" and they nodded.

There moved by the wind

was the purple sand of the key hole
the sunset gleaning the curved
the azure wave the somehow green glow
the swept sand and the knowing that
even as you died this thing would remain
always and impermeable, impervious to change
but ever altering, unknowable, yet known to all
that sought it, when they reached the beach

she took off her shoes, hurrying and
abandoning herself to the waves
to the bitter cold waves
to that which can only be sought and found
and fleeting is so perfect she cried
in her the myst and the surf were one
behind her the old men
looked on in a gentle haze
they promptly sat on the soft violet sand
as they had sat before so long ago
so many miles ago in the snow
on the mount, on the prairie
above the river, in ole new york

Drying on the shore, she checked her phone, it was becoming difficult to see, the spray of the ocean had coated it in a salty gleam. The old men sat as ever looking out to the sea, it was ever so. They had made it, all three. She quietly gathered her things, the light bowing to night, the fog beginning and originating from the breath of soaring redwood gods exhaled and came rolling in, off the hills, off, onto the trees, off toward her, toward the ocean, obscuring the cliffs, the jutting rock formations, the sky, washing the memories of years and years away. Back under and through the gaping mouth of the old trees, she went to the car, taking a final glance back at the beach but the fog opaque and hardening, washed over her. All that ever was, was gray again, was lost. There is no looking back only forward, there was no recovery of moment, of time, of place, of what and who you were an hour, a minute, a second before.

She opened the door and sat down in the empty space that became the car.

When her hand moved to the shift, she felt something curious move across her wrist. Something cool and smooth as glass and it was as though she could hear the sand shift and settle like rain. She flipped the wipers on as it came suddenly, a drenching downpour, and forced the pouring rain from her view, puddles of murky brown sand welled up and the road sank under the heaving burden of the sky.

'The headlights will point the way,' she thought, 'the headlights will point the way south.'

And aft in the mirror a lightning fissure strike carried over the road, beyond the trees, out onto the beach, two mounds of neon stinking blue smoke rose, leftovers for the yardbull's common thoughts returned like the bloated leather vulture scraps on bounty hunter boot sheen that oil the 600 miles of *El Camino Real* and it never goes cold.

This here thread grown forward and backward a hundred old odd years.

Some questions are solved in the parallel realities we build, some never and then some more just disappear. What and where and how—look left and right—does time ever go but for her and forever and us, there's nothing, but nothing, and once she hit the highway, no remains.

Gotovi Smo

About the Author

Tom Pescatore can sometimes be seen wandering along the Walt Whitman bridge or down the sidewalks of Philadelphia's old Skid Row. He's scratched out poems in the mountains of the North Cascades, on California's rocky coast and under pink desert skies over the Rio Grande, he might have left a few behind to mark his trail. He has published a poetry collection *Go On, Breathe Freely!* (2017) and writes the New Union from Junction City Comics. He claims ownership of a poetry blog: amagicalmistake.blogspot.com.

Acknowledgements

Parts and rearrangements of poems that appear in this novella first appeared in *Hollow*, *Pea River Journal*, *Mad Swirl*, *Westview*.

www.ingramcontent.com/pod-product-compliance
Lightning Source LLC
Chambersburg PA
CBHW072302130726
47910CB00012B/2415